34,420

MF
MAR

Martin, Lee

Too sane a murder

BNT DQS

DISCARD

DATE			
JAN 24	AUG 2	JUL 13 1999	
FEB 18	MAY 6	AUG 08 2000	
MAR 11	MAY 10	OCT 14 2000	
MAR 19	JUN 1	DEC 19 2000	
APR 11	SEP	JUL 2 3 2004	
APR 25	OCT 13		
MAY 31	MAR 3		
JUN 5	JUL 11		

Too
Sane a
Murder

LEE MARTIN

Too Sane a Murder

St. Martin's Press
New York

Library of Congress Cataloging in Publication Data

Martin, Lee, 1943–
    Too sane a murder.

    I. Title.
PS3563.A7249T6 1984   813'.54   84-13023
ISBN 0-312-80901-8

First Edition
10 9 8 7 6 5 4 3 2 1

To my parents and my children.
Thanks for the patience.

This book is fiction. The fictitious Fort Worth Police Department, the fictitious Tarrant County Jail, and the fictitious Tarrant County District Attorney's Office are in no way intended to represent the real-life Fort Worth Police Department, the real-life Tarrant County Jail, or the real-life Tarrant County District Attorney's Office. In particular I should note that although the isolation cell herein described is a real cell in a real jail, and I have really seen and smelled it, it is not located in Tarrant County, Texas.

The bullet hole in the elevator, on the other hand, is real.

No character in this book is intended to represent any real person in any real organization. Olead Baker, like Deb Ralston, came completely out of my own head.

And perhaps that says something about me.

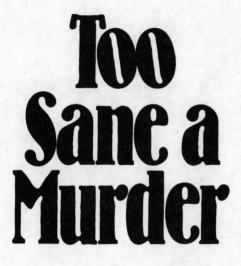

Too
Sane a
Murder

1

He wanted his bag of marbles.

That's what he told me.

Picture this. There are four people dead in the house and two—at least two—that ought to be there that we haven't found yet, and here is a twenty-six-year-old man asking for his bag of marbles.

And he wasn't even retarded. That wasn't what was wrong with him.

The first time he told me his name I thought he said Lee. The second time I thought he said Olee, and the third time he spelled it: O–L–E–A–D. He pronounced it Oh-leed.

I told him I'd never heard that name before, and he said that most people hadn't and he guessed it was a family name.

Later, he asked me what I was doing.

"I'm doing a crime scene," I answered.

"Looks to me like somebody's already done that," he said, and snickered. Then he said, "That wasn't funny, was it?"

"No," I told him, "that wasn't funny."

It was about as unfunny as anything I'd ever seen or

heard in my life. A neighbor had called the police emergency number about 3:00 A.M. to say he thought he'd heard a shot in the house next door. A uniform man went out there, and then homicide detectives, and then they called the major case squad.

Which was where I came in.

Captain Millner met me outside, his hands in the pockets of his gray overcoat and his shoulders hunched over against the wind. It was a cold, blustery, December?—January?—night; to be precise, it was 3:45 A.M. on January the first, New Year's Day. I was glad we had skipped the partying, and I had a hunch I wasn't going to be sitting in front of the television set at ten o'clock watching the Rose Parade, as is our usual New Year's Day habit.

Captain Millner—and no, I don't call him Scott and why should I? He's twenty years older than I am; he was a cop when I was in kindergarten; and he's proud of his rank and his position as head of the detective bureau. He's a big man, Scott Millner, maybe six foot six and two hundred thirty pounds, and he still gets his hair cut once a week just as he has done all his life. He looks like a cop.

Lieutenant Hollister—him I do call Gary—is the head of homicide. He's a small, foxy-looking man with curly red hair and a penchant for practical jokes, but right now he was home in bed with flu. Which was why it was Captain Millner who told me there were four known dead inside.

I said I already knew that; the dispatcher had told me when she called me out. He asked me if I'd ever seen shotgun killings before and I said yes, of course I had, and reminded him I had been a cop for fifteen years. He looked tiredly toward the sprawling brick house, where every light seemed to be on, and said, "I've seen them before too. But never four at once, never until now. I'd like to have that doctor up here, let her have a look at this."

Of course I asked what doctor, and he answered, "The one that said it was safe for the kid to come home. Some shrink named Susan Braun, now. This is the third time they've sent him home. The first time I was a lieutenant in uniform division. One of my men got the call."

The kid hadn't raised sand at home, that first time, Millner told me. The call was to the restroom of the library. That was the old library, the one on Throckmorton right across the street from the police station. It was old then; it's closed now, and the building is for sale. Anyhow, the kid—he was seventeen then—was buck naked, washing his jeans and shirt in the restroom sink. When the patrolman asked him why, he smiled angelically and answered, "They got dirty."

"How'd they get dirty?" the patrolman asked, making conversation in hopes of keeping the kid quiet until somebody got there with a set of jail coveralls. You can't take a naked seventeen-year-old across a downtown street, especially not at two o'clock in the afternoon.

Well, there was this cat.

The kid didn't like cats.

It developed he hadn't even touched the cat, that day; he'd just seen it crossing Throckmorton. No telling where it came from; most likely somebody had dumped it out of a car at a restaurant. People do things like that.

But when the kid saw the cat it made him feel dirty, so he was washing his clothes. He'd been trying to figure out how to get in the sink himself, but he hadn't quite worked that out yet. It would have been quite a feat if he had managed it. The sink was made for washing hands, and the kid, at seventeen, was over six feet tall.

Oh, yeah.

It was the women's restroom he was in.

Two years later they tried again to send him home. Now mind you, the doctor wasn't claiming he'd been cured. Cure, for schizophrenia, probably doesn't exist. Control, yes, but not permanent, one-hundred-percent-guaranteed cure. But the doctor wasn't even claiming he was controlled. He was just saying it was important for the kid not to lose all contact with the real world.

He was bigger that time, and stronger, and wilder. That

time the call was to his house, and he'd demolished it. Just about totally. Have you ever, Millner demanded, seen a platform rocker shoved through a sheetrock wall? All the way through, so that it was lying on its back in a pile of crumbled sheetrock on the double bed in the next room?

It took four men to fight him down and get him into the patrol car that time. He didn't go to the state hospital in Terrell, because the Bakers had money—enough money to put him in a private place, where he could be kept decently out of sight in comfort.

But that time the private hospital kept him a long time.

"I don't know how long he's been back," Captain Millner told me, trying to light a cigarette in the gusty wind. "I didn't even recognize him at first—the address is different, and the names don't jibe. The kid doesn't look the same as he did, and he's even using a different first name. Back then he called himself Jimmy. Still the same last name on him, but not on anybody else in the house. Best as I can tell, his daddy's dead and his mama had remarried, some fellow name of Jack Carson, and had two more children."

"And that's who's dead?" I asked, feeling sick. "The parents and kids?" The adults, too often, bring homicide on themselves, but no cop ever gets used to dead kids.

Besides, I was getting ready to be a grandmother, and that maybe had me a little hypersensitive.

Millner gave up on the cigarette; there was too much wind. He pitched it, still unlit, onto the sidewalk. "The parents, yes," he said. "The kids, probably, but we haven't found them yet. Two other adults; we haven't identified them for sure. And we don't know if they had any kids. He says no, but I don't know what that's worth."

"Haven't found them?" My mind was still on the kids.

My face must have mirrored the incredulity I felt, for Millner spat into the shrubbery and said, "You'll see when you get inside." He turned to look toward the house. "There's no real doubt the kid did it."

"Then why'd you call me?" The major case squad becomes involved with an investigation only if it promises to be extremely complicated or time-consuming. A solved homicide—even one with four, or six, corpses—does not fall into that category.

"I don't know," Millner said slowly. "Damn it, I don't *know*."

He didn't need to translate that, not to me or any other experienced cop. What he meant was that there was something wrong and he didn't know what it was; he couldn't put a finger on it; and so despite his certainty that the kid had pulled the trigger, and the fact that the case would never go to trial with the kid already a diagnosed schizophrenic, he still wanted a full investigation.

I nodded, and I had one foot on the first step going up to the front door when Millner, behind me, added a little too casually, "Oh yeah. The kid's still in the house."

I turned.

Of course Millner knows just as well as I do that the suspect is never, but never, allowed to stay in the place where the crime took place while the investigation is going on.

So I didn't ask why. I waited for Millner to tell me.

"He asked to stay until Brenda and Jeffrey—that's the missing kids—turn up. He's docile enough now; he's burned off whatever kind of a fit made him do it." Millner took off his glasses and rubbed the bridge of his nose with his thumb and two fingers. "If he was going to trial I couldn't get away with it. But he's not. I want him to stay around. I want everybody to listen to what he says. Oh, and Deb. I asked for you especially. I think he'll relate to you. I think you'll remind him of his doctor."

"You think, or you hope?" I asked sourly.

He grinned. "All right. I hope. But see what you can get out of him, Deb, without him balking about answering. He's had a Miranda warning. Not that it matters in this case."

"I'll try," I said dubiously. Nuts I do not like and everybody who knows me knows that. But I went on up the stairs, and the patrolman guarding the front entrance, standing in the wind with the fur collar of his jacket turned up around his neck, caught hold of the polished brass knob with his leather gloves to open the door for me.

The entry hall was warm and bright. The light gray carpet was clean except for the leaves and mud tracked in by police and the crew from the medical examiner's office—an investigator and a transport crew only, because both medical examiners had flu. On my right was a walnut hall table, with a brass tray and two brass candlesticks on it. The candlesticks had holly wreathed around them, and fat beeswax candles in them, and on the brass tray was a brass bowl filled with shiny red apples so thickly waxed you'd never dare eat one of them.

The living room had six-foot-long pearl gray twin sofas facing each other, looking as if no one ever sat on them. There were walnut end tables with big lamps on them, but there was no coffee table. I saw no books, no magazines, no newspapers, no ash trays, nothing to indicate people lived in the house. There was no television, no stereo—conscientiously, I reminded myself such things might be in the den. There was a formal fireplace with three pristine logs in it, and more candles on the white mantel. One side wall was almost entirely filled with a white flocked tree, formally decorated with silver balls in three sizes, silver swags of tinsel, and tiny independently twinkling silver lights.

Still plugged in and twinkling.

Obviously, these people left their Christmas decorations up until New Year's Day. I never do; I feel as if they're a fire hazard, but I'm aware that a lot of people disagree with me.

I wondered why nobody had unplugged the lights. Then I wondered why I didn't, and I headed for the outlet, and a crime scene technician said quickly, "Uh-uh." I looked at him, and he explained, "We haven't taken pictures in here yet."

When I arrive at a crime scene, the first thing I like to

do is walk through the building. To make sure I remember not to touch anything until it's been photographed and, if necessary, fingerprinted, I always keep my hands clasped behind my back. Just about everybody who's really aware of the value of physical evidence does that.

From the front of the house, I moved on through to the dining room, which was completely clean, untouched. There was no tablecloth on the walnut table, and the long walnut buffet had a silver epergne of crysanthemums on it. All the wood I saw was walnut. This was old money, I guessed; walnut furniture tends to be old money.

The breakfast room showed signs of a meal—plates, five of them, Royal Doulton china and Francis I silver. In the breakfast room, yet. Dried eggs and grits on the plates, and toast crumbs. There was a faint smell of bacon in the air, and a strong smell of coffee.

Breakfast.

Some people have a special breakfast at midnight on New Year's Eve. But in Fort Worth, Texas, that usually includes black-eyed peas. There was no sign here of black-eyed peas.

That could present a little mystery, I thought. Why had they been eating breakfast—a perfectly ordinary breakfast—sometime before three o'clock in the morning?

I walked on toward the kitchen and then looked back. I had acquired a tail.

He was tall, maybe six-two. He had blue eyes and short wavy brown hair and white teeth, which were immediately evident because he was smiling tentatively at me. He looked the complete preppy; you would expect to find him on a tennis court, with a good tan and white shorts and two or three girls clinging to him. In fact, he had no tan at all; he was wearing faded blue jeans, an orange plaid shirt, and cowboy boots; and of course he was alone.

Unless you want to count the patrolman who was silently following him.

"Who're you?" he asked, in a rather pleasant baritone.

"Deb Ralston," I told him. "I'm a detective."

"Are you?" he asked interestedly. "That's funny. You don't look like a detective. You look like—like—like somebody's sweet little aunt. No offense," he added hastily.

I agreed there was no offense. I told him I was several people's aunt, and a few people's mother, but I was a detective, too. And then I asked him who he was.

When we got the Olead sorted out, I asked if that was really his name.

He said it was his middle name, and he'd decided to start using it because he thought Jim was an ordinary kind of name. "There's such a lot of Jims," he pointed out, and asked me if I didn't think Olead was a better name.

"I don't know," I told him. "I never thought about it."

"Of course you didn't," he said gleefully, a child catching a grown-up out. "You already told me you'd never heard the name before. So you couldn't think about it." He snickered again.

For a moment I felt annoyed, and then, suddenly, I realized what he really was, inside the too-cool exterior. Without stopping to think the question might antagonize him, might shut off his stream of talk, I impulsively asked, "Olead, were you fifteen the first time you flipped out?"

"How'd you guess that?" he demanded, and then he said, "Oh, I know. Somebody told you, right?"

"No, nobody told me," I said. "It's because you act fifteen."

"How do I act fifteen?" he asked suspiciously.

"I'd rather not say."

"No, tell me," he urged. "I won't get mad."

"It's typical of a fifteen-year-old in a touchy situation," I explained, "to make inappropriate jokes and laugh about them. I think it's some sort of attempt to defuse the situation."

"Inappropriate." His face darkened, momentarily became adult. "Yeah, my shrink says that. She says I've always got to make my actions appropriate to the situation, whether

I want to or not. But how do I know what's appropriate now? Do you know what's in there?" His voice was raw with suppressed violence, with some emotion I couldn't read, as he glanced in the direction of the den.

"No," I said. "Would you like to show me?"

"No. But I will."

He led me into a clean kitchen, which had an electric drip coffeepot on the counter, half full of dark old coffee. There were a few grease spatters not wiped off the almond enamel of the cooktop, and a sink full of water held a single frying pan, a spatula, a saucepan, and a blender jar.

A breakfast bar divided the kitchen from the den. Olead paused there, so that I was standing with the end of the breakfast bar beside my left hand. He was between my right side and the opposite wall, and both of us were looking into the next room.

The den was—or should have been—a slightly more relaxed place than the living room. It had a creamy ceramic tile floor instead of the gray carpet of the rest of the house. A brown couch effectively dividing the room in half sat with its back toward the kitchen and its face toward the big fireplace, where burned-out ashes and a faint pine scent told of recent use. There were a couple of brown vinyl recliner chairs, and on top of the big console television and stereo were a few newspapers and magazines. Empty cups sat on the end tables and coffee table; apparently the victims had come in here after leaving the breakfast room.

One body—a middle-aged man in a red plaid shirt, blue jeans, and worn cowboy boots—was sprawled back in one of the recliners. His face appeared astonished. "That's Jack," Olead said gravely, seeing the direction of my gaze. "He's— he was—my—my mother's husband."

"Your stepfather," I said.

"Well, yeah," Olead agreed.

The other man was near the television, and his hand gripped a shotgun, an old double-barreled over-and-under shotgun and rifle combination. He'd been ready to fight back, I thought, but he'd died instantly. I was sure of that because his grip was tight in that cadaveric spasm that happens only in absolutely instant death, that death grip that is so hard for laymen to distinguish from normal rigor mortis. I knew that it would take two or three people to pry from his hand the weapon he had been gripping when the blast hit his face. There wasn't much left to say what he'd looked like, but his belt buckle said "Jake." He was wearing a khaki shirt and khaki pants, and he was shod in combat boots.

"I guess that's Jake," Olead confirmed. "I mean, I can't tell by looking, but nobody else would be wearing Jake's belt. He—he was Jack's brother. I called him Uncle Jake, but he really wasn't any kin to me." His gaze shifted. "That's Aunt Edith. Jake's wife."

Edith had graying red hair. Her expression was one to glance at and look away fast; unlike the men, she hadn't died instantly. She'd tried to reach the phone. Probably she had reached it; she may have had it off the hook, before some hand—Olead's hand?—jerked the modular plug out of the jack.

She had been wearing, was still wearing, a dark calico duster over a blue nylon gown, and blue chenille bedroom scuffs. A wad of pink Kleenex was sticking out of the pocket of the duster, and even over the odor of death and terror in the room I could smell a faint hint of Vicks Vaporub.

Edith's cold wouldn't be troubling her now.

The last body was beside the patio door; she'd tried to run, I thought, but hadn't gotten the door open before the shot hit her in a wide pattern, which said it had been fired from a good distance. She was dressed in tailored wool slacks and a shirt, a red shirt now, though it might have been white to start with. I couldn't tell. It would be red now anyway. Her neatly styled hair was blonde, light champagne blonde, the fashionable shade this year, and her true red fingernail polish was perfectly smooth and unchipped. It was impossible to judge what her terror-contorted face had looked like in life.

No, that wasn't quite the last body. There was one more, just beside her feet. I turned to look at Olead.

"My mother," he said emotionlessly, a flat statement of fact. Then he turned to look at the other body, which was no more now than an unidentifiable mass of bloody fur. "The cat was Brenda's."

"Who's Brenda?"

"My sister. She's four. We haven't found her yet."

"You don't like cats, do you, Olead?" I asked casually.

"Not much," he said. "But I don't dislike them, at least not enough to go around killing them. Oh." He looked at me. "You're talking about when I was schizo. I was scared of them, but I'm not now."

"Not schizo, or not scared of cats?"

"Not schizo *or* scared of cats. Did you see that?"

I nodded. "Yes, I saw that." *That* was a shotgun, a twelve-gauge Remington, leaning against the wall opposite the end of the breakfast bar, very near Olead's right hand.

"Why do you think it's there?"

I surveyed the scene again. "I'd say somebody left it there. What do you think?"

"I think it's a dumb place to leave a gun. Are you scared of me?"

"No. Should I be?"

He jerked his head contemptuously in the direction of the patrolman. "He is. He woke me up at three-fifteen this morning hammering on the door, and he and I together found the bodies. He's been following me around ever since, and I'll bet he hasn't had his hand off his gun five minutes. Look at him."

I looked. The patrolman was probably four years younger than Olead. His silver name plate said "Shea"; his face at the moment was brick red; and yes, his right hand was resting on his gun. Well, I could understand how he might be a little nervous of somebody who could create the carnage in that room, but he didn't have to let the suspect notice his nerves. "Shea," I said softly, "take a walk."

"But I—"

"Shea," I said a little less softly, "take a walk."

"Yes, ma'am," Shea said, his face even redder and now somewhat blotchy. He stalked off in the direction of the living room, his movements jerky with rage. Apparently I had made an enemy. I didn't much care, not if he was that easily made an enemy.

I turned my attention back to Olead. "Now, to return to our conversation. Should I be?"

"I'm a lot bigger than you." That was perfectly true. I am five feet two inches tall and not a whole lot overweight. Olead, as I think I have said, was about six feet two inches tall and not a whole lot underweight.

"But I know judo," I answered, not very truthfully. The fact is that I took a six-week judo course ten years ago, at my husband's insistence.

"I'm real close to a shotgun."

"I'm even closer to a thirty-eight. And it's loaded. Is the shotgun?" I knew this kind of game playing; again Olead had turned fifteen. He was playing his own variant of the my-dad's-bigger-than-your-dad game.

He looked at the shotgun without touching it. "How should I know if it's loaded or not?" he asked bitterly. "Jack let me look at it last night, and he said if I stayed well he'd teach me how to use it next year, but he said he didn't think it was quite the right time yet."

Neat. He'd explained why his fingerprints would of course be on the shotgun, without waiting to find out if they were. "Did your real dad tell you anything about guns?" I asked.

"Yeah. He told me I could learn to shoot when I was sixteen."

"Did you?"

"Ah, come on," Olead said disgustedly. "Who do you think is going to teach a schizo to use a shotgun? Another schizo?"

"Maybe," I said mildly. "Do you sleep in your boots?"

"Of course I don't sleep in my boots. Why would I want to sleep in my boots?" The voice scornful now. He was running a full gamut of emotions. He was working at that, working at not looking at the bodies.

"Well, you said Shea woke you up, but you didn't say anything about dressing. Why don't you show me where you were sleeping when he woke you up?"

"This way." Apparently no longer interested in the shotgun, he escorted me out into the hall which led to the left, toward bedrooms, and to the right, back toward the living room. "This is where I sleep."

I followed him inside. I could take his word that he slept here, but I wasn't sure he did anything else. The walls, white and clean, were as impersonal as those in a hotel, if not more so. There were no pictures, no posters, nothing individual. He had a bachelor chest, a desk with a bookshelf over it, and a Hollywood bed, three-quarter size, with no headboard or footboard. It had a white spread, a blue blanket, white sheets, all rumpled as if someone had gotten out of bed in a hurry. A pair of blue cotton pajamas were folded on the foot of the bed. "That's what I had on," Olead said. "Shea told me to get dressed and leave the pajamas there. He said the lab would want them. Can they do that?"

"Do what?" I was unfolding the pajamas.

"Take my clothes. Can they do that?"

"Yep."

"Without even having a search warrant?"

"You don't need a search warrant to search the scene of a crime," I answered absently. Yes, there it was, what Shea had doubtless noticed, a brownish smear on the right sleeve and right shoulder.

"What's that?" Olead asked, stepping closer to me, his voice alarmed. "That wasn't there when I went to bed. What is it?"

"Blood, probably," I answered, laying the shirt back on the bed.

"*What?* That's impossible! I *never* touched—the bodies

—not ever!" Consciously or not, he was pleading with me now to believe him, to be on his side. "Look, that man, Captain Whatever-his-name-is, he thinks I did it, he thinks I killed my mother, and I didn't, I would—*what's that?*" His agitated pacing had turned him around, and he had spotted something behind his bedroom door, something Shea should have seen and probably hadn't. "That's not mine!"

He wasn't far short of panic now, and I said, "Calm down, son. Just calm down."

"That isn't mine," he said again, in a slightly calmer tone.

"All right. It isn't yours. Do you know whose it is?"

"Uh-uh." He was staring, wide-eyed, at the weapon. "No—I—wait a minute. It might—maybe it's my dad's. Was my dad's. He had a—a real old shotgun. Is that a shotgun? My mom might've kept it. I—I—" He looked at me. "I'm sorry. I don't remember your name."

"Deb."

"My doctor says I'm not allowed to call grown-ups by their first name. Said, that is. My old doctor said that. He's dead."

He spoke in just the tone a boy might use to repeat boring instructions from a parent or teacher, and I replied, "Don't worry about that. Everybody calls me Deb."

"Deb," he said, trying it out. Then he said, "Deb, that's not mine. And I didn't put it there."

His shock looked real. But so did the blood on his pajamas, and I felt sure that very officious rookie Shea had not let him near the bodies after they were officially discovered. I looked at him, and as I looked I saw him rub at his right shoulder. "Does it hurt?" I asked.

"Does what hurt? My shoulder?" He looked puzzled. "Yeah, it kind of hurts, like a bruise maybe. I can't think of anything I've done to it, though."

"Mind if I look at it?" I asked, working at sounding casual.

"It'll be okay," he said. "I probably just slept on it wrong."

"Probably," I agreed, "but I'd still like a look at it, if you don't mind." In order to give him time to decide whether to cooperate or argue, I turned to glance over the books on the shelf above his desk. There were several books on mental illness, several books on nutrition of the health-food store variety, an apparently much-read copy of *The Eden Express*. He had a small selection of science fiction and a few innocuous mysteries.

Hearing him moving around behind me, I asked, "How long have you been home from the hospital?"

"Six months," he said. That was a little surprise, with the room still looking as impersonal as it did. Even the books, except for the six or eight about mental illness and nutrition, were the type you'd put in a guest room in case the visitor wanted to read.

"Hey," he said crossly, "you want to look at my shoulder or not? It's a little cool with this shirt half off."

I turned. There was a red mark on his shoulder, one that eventually was going to turn into a bad bruise. I'd seen the identical mark on my own shoulder often enough, when I was learning to fire a shotgun. "Okay," I said. "It'll be sore, but you're not really hurt."

He started to button the plaid flannel shirt, and I sat down casually in his desk chair, leaving him no place to sit unless he wanted to park on the bed.

"Now, son," I said, "would you like to tell me the truth?"

2

He didn't panic.

He didn't shout, and he didn't go for the shotgun.

He looked at me silently, and his face for a moment looked older than fifteen and older than twenty-six. Then he sat down, not on the bed but on the floor, in one graceful fluid motion that began with his left leg bending at the knee and ended with his feet crossed in front of him on the floor. He looked up at me. "Starting from when?" he asked.

And I thought, is it going to be this easy? "Starting from last night," I answered. "Suppertime, how's that?"

He shrugged. "Suppertime. Okay. Jake and Edith were spending the week here. I don't like to call them Uncle Jake and Aunt Edith, is it okay if I don't?" I nodded. "They're from Arkansas. You knew that, didn't you?" I shook my head, remembering the captain had said the bodies weren't definitely identified. "Okay," he said. "Well, they are, and they were spending the week here. I already said that, didn't I?"

He scratched his head and went on. "We had waffles with creamed tuna on them for supper, with green peas in the creamed tuna, and Brenda was whining a little because she doesn't like peas. I don't know why; I like peas; but she doesn't. So Edith said proper children don't have to be made to eat, and Jack got mad and told Brenda she had to eat them like it or not. So she started crying and ate the peas and threw up, I guess because of the crying, and Jack spanked her and sent her to bed. Only of course she couldn't sleep in her bed because Jake and Edith have it, and she was on a pallet at the foot of her own bed, and she wanted to sleep in my room because she said Edith—she said Aunt Edith, of course—didn't smell good, and Jack spanked her again, and she said she meant Aunt Edith's medicine didn't smell good. And I said of course she could sleep in my room, because it's really her room anyway—she's been sharing Jeffrey's room since I got home—and I said I'd get Jack's sleeping bag and sleep on the floor. Then Edith said that was totally unsuitable, Brenda sharing a room with a *man*. I swear, that woman's a dingbat—my sister, for crying out loud, and only four years old!"

He stopped. "You're not supposed to say bad things about dead people, are you?"

"Was she a dingbat?"

"Yeah, she was a dingbat."

"Then say it. Anyhow, what happened next?"

"Then Jack said I couldn't have the sleeping bag anyway because he wanted it himself because he and Jake were leaving about one-thirty to go hunting. So I said then let her have the bed and I'd go sleep on the couch. Edith sniffed and said she hated to put anybody out, and Mother said I couldn't sleep on the couch because they were going to be having a party later on. And Jack said Brenda could sleep where she was told to sleep, on a folded-up quilt on the floor. And he told her to go there right that minute. After she went to lie down, I told Jack the floor gets kind of hard, and I used to have a sleeping bag of my own, if it was still around. Mother told me I had to sleep in my own room, and I said well, at least Brenda could have my sleeping bag, if it was still around."

"Was it?"

"Yeah, Jack said he didn't mean to be so cross but he was worrying about money. He said he thought the old one might still be in the attic somewhere, and I got up there and looked and managed to find it. So I put it in the dryer to warm it up and try to get some of the dust off, and then I took it in there to Brenda. She was still sort of crying, you know how little kids do when they're through crying but don't know how to stop, and I told her she could have my sleeping bag and I'd sit with her until she went to sleep. She asked me if she could really have the sleeping bag for keeps, and I told her yes and showed her how the zipper works. Then I told her to hippity-hop in and go to sleep. I was sitting in there on the floor with her and Edith prissed in sniffing and said if I would be so good as to excuse her, she wished to retire. I asked her if that meant she wanted to go to bed, and she said yes, and I asked her why didn't she just say so, and she sniffed again and said she wouldn't expect *me* to understand. So I said, 'Oh, I understand, auntie.' She doesn't—didn't—like me to call her auntie. Brenda giggled, and Edith sniffed a few more times, and I told Brenda to sleep tight, and then I went to my room." He shook his head. "Edith was a dingbat," he said again.

If his account was accurate, I had to agree. Edith sounded like a dingbat. But I was also aware that the mentally ill, even more than the rest of us, tend to see things only from their own point of view. "What happened then?" I asked. "You mentioned a party. Was there one?"

"Sort of. Not a very good one. I didn't want to go to it. I wanted to go to the Water Garden. But Mother said that was absurd, nobody was going to take me to the Water Garden after dark on New Year's Eve, especially with the weather turning nasty. And I can't drive, you know."

I told him I didn't know, and he said, "Well, I can't. But anyhow, the party was miserable. People expect booze at New Year's Eve parties, and when they found out there wasn't any they tended to stay just long enough to be polite and then kind of, you know, drift away, saying they had to get home to their baby-sitters, or they had promised to look in on another party, or something."

"Why wasn't there any booze?"

"Oh, Mother thought it wouldn't be good for me to have it around. And then she made a big production out of how inconvenient it all was, and I couldn't get it across to her that I really didn't care whether she had it around or not, I wasn't going to drink anyway. Look," he said earnestly, "schizophrenia is something that happened to me. I didn't do it. I didn't choose for it to happen. But my head has been messed up enough. I certainly don't want it avoidably messed up."

"What time did everybody leave the party?" I asked.

"I don't know. I went to bed before it was over. I guess there were still about twelve people here, but I got real sleepy."

"Did you know any of the twelve?"

"I didn't know anybody that came. I wasn't paying much attention anyway. They were friends of Jack, mostly. Some of them I remember from before my dad died, even before I got sick, but—I had a lot of shock treatment. And even if I hadn't, that was a long time ago. And I'm not good at remembering names."

"What kind of things happened at the party?" I asked. I could see no reason any of this could matter, but I was on a fishing expedition.

"Oh, just people talking and that sort of stuff. I remember Jack said something about him and Jake going out in the morning real early to hunt rabbits and this one man said he might like to go too, but why so early, on New Year's Day at that, and Jack laughed and said, 'Oh, that was something we used to do when we were kids. New Year's Day is the best time of all to go hunting, because the crazies are all in bed sleeping it off.' And then that guy looked at me real fast and then looked away, you know that look, the one that says, 'Don't look now but that guy's crazy but don't let him know you know.'"

"Did that make you mad at Jack?"

"Not at Jack. He didn't mean it the way it sounded. He meant the drunks. He always refers to drunks as crazies. He always has. But I was kind of pissed at the other guy, because of the way he looked at me, so superior, as if I had gotten schizo on purpose. I mean he was looking at me like that and I didn't even know who he was. And I wouldn't have cared if he'd just stared, like he was curious. People *are* curious. That doesn't bother me."

"How long have you known Jack?" I asked.

"All my life. He was a friend of Dad."

"Did it make you mad, him marrying your mother after your father died?"

"You're making noises like a shrink, you know it?" Olead protested.

"Sorry," I said. "Didn't mean to be. I just wanted to know."

"Anyhow, your chronology's off. Mother married Jack before Dad died. Mother and Dad were divorced eight years ago and Mother married Jack about six months later."

"Why? The divorce, I mean?"

He shrugged. "How do I know? I wasn't there. Dad told me it wasn't my fault and didn't have anything to do with me, and he told me not to feel harsh toward Jack, that Jack had been a friend to me and would keep on being one. But he told me not ever to out-and-out *give* anything to Mother or Jack. He said later on when I was in a position to, I could help them all I wanted, but to keep strings attached—keep things in my name."

"Why's that?" I asked, wondering why the man had expected his schizophrenic son ever to be in a position to help his mother and stepfather anyway.

"Oh, because Mother likes—liked to gamble. And Jack did, too. And neither one of them was any good at it." He looked at me, his expression puzzled. "What does this have to do with what happened last night?"

"I don't know," I told him. "That's what I'm trying to

figure out myself. It's funny, I didn't see any sign at all of a party when I got here. What happened after that conversation? Did everybody go home?"

"I told you I went to bed. There were still about twelve people here, and they were wandering back and forth between the living room and the den. I got real sleepy, and I went to bed. But I can tell you why there's no sign of a party. Mother never leaves stuff overnight; she always cleans up and puts everything away before she goes to bed, no matter how late it is. So I don't know when she went to bed, or even *if* she did. I don't really think she did, because those clothes were the same ones—" His face tightened momentarily, and he wiped his eyes with the back of his hand. He swallowed and said, "I went to sleep. And when I woke up that policeman was banging on the door. Of course I didn't know he was a policeman; I just knew there was somebody at the door, and I kept expecting Jack to get up and go see who it was. But he didn't, so I did."

"Why did you expect him to, if he was supposed to leave about one-thirty?"

"I didn't remember that right then. Anyway, I didn't know what time it was. I was really out of it; I felt too sleepy to move, but I finally got up anyway."

"And you didn't go to the den?"

"No reason to." That was true, of course; the direct route from his bedroom to the front door didn't go through the den. "I went through the hall into the living room and opened the door, and that policeman—Shea—said they had a report of a shot fired in the house, and was everything okay? I told him if there'd been a shot fired I'd have heard it, and there hadn't been. He asked me if I minded if he looked around, and I said no, come on in. And he walked through the house taking the same route you took when you first came in, and when we turned on the den light—" He swallowed. "Then I had to run to the bathroom, and Shea tried to stop me, and I put my hand over my mouth and then Shea let go of me and I got to the bathroom and—I threw up."

"Did you flush?"

He stared at me. "I was too sick. Shea flushed. Then he went in my room and walked around in it a minute and then he went back out in the hall and told me to go in there and change clothes. I already told you about that. But that's what happened last night. That's all I know."

"Okay. I want to ask you some questions now." Conscientiously, I gave him another Miranda warning, and he reminded me "that captain" already did that and he'd already signed it. "You said you didn't eat anything after supper. Is that right?"

"Well, I ate some chips and drank a diet Dr. Pepper, but that's all."

"Diet?"

"I can't handle much sugar," he explained. "Wait a minute, I remember that's not all. I had one cup of punch. But I thought it tasted gross. I wasn't going to finish it, but Mother acted hurt about it, so I drank it and then I got the Dr. Pepper. I guess it was about thirty minutes later that I went to bed."

"You didn't get up later and eat breakfast?"

"When would I have eaten breakfast?"

"Somebody ate breakfast."

"That would be Jack and Jake. They would have eaten breakfast before they went hunting, and you could tell they were already dressed for that."

"Olead, there are five plates on that table."

"Well, Mother and Edith. Maybe the fifth was a serving plate." He sounded unconvinced.

"Olead, you got up and ate breakfast."

"No, I didn't."

"You got up and ate breakfast, and then the quarreling started again, and you picked up a shotgun that was out ready and waiting for somebody to go hunt rabbits, and then you started shooting."

"No, I didn't," he said. "Anyway, Jack would never load a shotgun before he got to where he was going to hunt."

"Somebody did."

"It wasn't Jack."

"Then maybe you loaded it yourself."

"I don't know how to load a shotgun."

"Olead, do you know why your shoulder's sore?"

"No, I don't," he said.

I looked at the shot gun in the corner. It was an old twelve-gauge Browning, pre-1920, probably, because there was no sign that it had ever had a serial number. It hadn't been well cared for, and as rusty as it was, it would never hold fingerprints. I could put it back for photographs to be taken later. I picked it up and sniffed at it, and the raw smell of gunpowder suggested it had been fired recently. I checked it, jacked three red plastic shells out onto the floor, checked it again. It was empty now. "Olead, undo your shirt again," I said.

Looking puzzled, he unbuttoned his shirt.

"Slide your right arm out of the sleeve," I said.

He slid his arm out of the sleeve.

"Now, look at your shoulder," I said. "You see that red mark?"

He looked at it. "Yeah."

I held the shotgun up to his shoulder and fitted the back of the stock against his shoulder. "That's what made that mark," I told him.

"That isn't true," he said, and reached for the shotgun.

"No," I said, moving it out of his reach, "I don't want you to touch it."

"I'm not going to fire it," he said impatiently. "I can't anyway, you took all the bullets out. I just want to—"

"I don't want you to touch it now," I said. I went to the door. "What evidence technicians have we got out here?" I asked.

"Me and Irene," Bob Castle called from the den. "Why?"

"Have you got a trace metal detection kit?"

"In the van, why?"

"Can you break away from what you're doing and bring it in here?"

"I guess."

"What's a trace metal detection kit?" Olead asked.

"It's going to tell me if you've fired a shotgun," I said, and then corrected myself. "No, it's going to tell me if you've held a shotgun lately."

"What's that going to prove?" Olead asked. "I told you I held one last night. I was looking at it."

Bob came in with two small dark gray plastic carrying cases. "Might as well get these both done at once," he said. "What's your name, bub?"

Olead flushed and answered stiffly, "My name is James Olead Baker." He spelled Olead and, for good measure, Baker.

"Okay, Baker, I'm going to spray this stuff on your hands and arms and face. It won't hurt. Are you right-handed or left-handed?"

"Right-handed. What is that stuff?"

"I don't know the name of it myself. But I can tell you how it works. When you touch metal, an infinitesimal trace of it stays on your skin. This chemical is very sensitive; when we put black light on it, it'll show us if you've touched metal lately, and what kind, and it'll show us the shape of whatever parts of the metal you were touching. Understand?"

"Uh-huh."

Bob reached up and turned off the overhead light. In the darkness, he turned on the ultraviolet light he held in his hand. In the darkness, Olead's hands, including his trigger finger and the side of his face where it might have rested against the metal insignia inlaid in the gun-stock, glowed eerily. Bob turned the light on again.

"What does that mean?" Olead asked, looking warily at his hands.

"It means you've held a shotgun or rifle in firing position in the last twelve hours," Bob told him.

"But I didn't," Olead said. "I'd remember if I did, and I didn't—what's that?"

"It's a gunpowder residue test," Bob said. "These are just plain cotton swabs. I'm going to put about three drops of two percent nitric acid on each one and swab your hands with it. Then we can find out if you've fired a gun. Hold out your hands."

"I haven't," Olead said, and held out his hands obediently. Then he asked, "Aren't you going to tell me what it says?"

"It has to go to the lab. I can't read this test."

"Oh," Olead said. "How long does that take?"

"About three weeks, unless we can get them to speed it up."

"Oh," Olead said again. "Then have I got to stay in jail three weeks, until it comes back?"

"In my opinion, bub, you're going to be staying in jail the rest of your life," Bob told him coldly, and left the room carrying both kits.

Olead, who had sat on the bed for the tests to be done, got off it and sat back down on the floor. "Deb," he said, "please try to understand this. I am not insane. I was insane for eleven years and I know how it affected me—I don't necessarily know how schizophrenia affects anybody else, but I know how it affected me. There has never been a time in my life when I would have done what was done in that room. I have been violent; I'm not denying that. I've tried to kill myself a lot of times, but I've never tried to kill anybody else. Any time I jumped anybody else was always the result of a sudden—snapping, is all I know how to call it—and then the attack would be purely physical and it would be aimed at one person, either the one person I was at that time blaming for the situation, or else just whoever was closest. If I had snapped like that last night, I probably would have gone for Edith, because all right, I admit I was pissed at Edith because she was bullying my sister and trying to bully me, only I don't bully that easy any more. But I would have gone for her with my hands, not with a shotgun. And the other thing is, I would have remembered. I always remembered. There were times I couldn't control what I did, and there were even times I couldn't figure out what was right and what was wrong, but I was always sorry later. I might start doing the same thing again as soon as I saw that person again even if I was sorry, but I didn't forget doing it. I didn't forget."

"Olead, was there ever a weapon at hand when you snapped?"

He thought about it. "No."

"And did you ever really hurt anybody else?"

He didn't have to think about that so long. "No," he answered instantly.

"But suppose you snapped, and there was a shotgun at hand, and all of a sudden there were people dead—would you be able to remember that? Or would you say that's not me, that's not a thing I would do, and blank it out of your mind?"

He shook his head. "I feel like hell," he said. "I feel shaky, and I haven't felt like this in months. But I don't feel like I snapped. I just feel like I've had too much Thorazine, which is silly because I'm not even taking Thorazine anymore. But I feel like hell physically, and that's all. I'm not having any schizophrenic symptoms, and God knows I know them. I don't know how that mark got on my shoulder, but I do know that I did not fire a shotgun last night. Besides, you haven't finished looking at the rest of the house. Will you let me show it to you?"

Apparently, he was through talking. "Yeah," I said, "show it to me."

We went past an open bathroom door. We went to a large bedroom that contained only a king-size bed and a triple dresser. "That's Mother and Jack's room," he said. "Not much furniture in it, wouldn't you agree?"

"No, there's not," I said.

"Here's why."

The third bedroom, at the front of the house, presented

about the most unbelievable sight I had ever seen in my life. It resembled nothing so much as the aftermath of a tornado, with everything in it pulled out, slung around, stood on end and on its side and piled on top of everything else. Furniture from other rooms had been hauled in and forced into the confusion. "Brenda and Jeffrey are somewhere under that, I think," he said. "I tried to get Shea to let me start moving stuff and look for them, but he wouldn't. I asked your captain the same thing, and he said they're dead and we'll get to them when we get to them. Well, I don't think they're dead. I think somebody wanted to barricade them in with all that stuff, so there'd be no chance of them being the ones to find—the others. I haven't worried about it too much, because it's not time for them to be waking up yet, and they both sleep pretty soundly. But Deb, do you think I could have done all that and not remembered it?"

I was silent. I was remembering what Captain Millner had told me—*have you ever seen a chair thrown through a sheetrock wall*—and I said, "I'm sorry, Olead, but yes. Yes, I do."

He made a helpless gesture with his hands. "I'm sorry too. I thought the system of justice in this country said a man is innocent until proven guilty. But you're asking me to prove myself innocent, and I can't do that. All I can do is tell you that I slept through the shooting in the den, which is right next to my bedroom, and I slept through all the commotion in here, which is right across the hall from my bedroom, and I can't tell you how or why. I haven't killed anybody." He sat down on the floor in the hall. "Please find my brother and sister," he said simply.

Bob, who apparently had heard him, called, "Deb, we're through with pictures for now and aren't going to try for fingerprints in there, so if you want to start to move stuff around, that's okay." He came out into the hall and set a camera and a fingerprint kit down beside me. "We're swamped. It would help a lot if you could do that room."

"Okay," I said. I had been a crime scene technician myself, years ago, and I still did my own crime scenes sometimes when ident was really busy. It wasn't as if I didn't know how.

Apparently I was going to have to prove to Olead, even if not to a jury, that he had done it himself. So experimentally I got out black fingerprint powder and a Zephyr brush—I always work with a Zephyr brush—and started to dust the legs of a chair that stuck grotesquely out in midair. I stopped abruptly and turned to Olead. "Do you have any gloves?" I asked.

"Yeah, sure."

"Get them for me, would you?" I followed him as he went back to his room and fished the gloves out of the pocket of a quilted jacket. I took them back in the other room. "Look at the weave of the gloves," I said.

He looked. "So?" he said questioningly.

"Now look at this chair leg." I pointed. "That's glove marks, Olead. The lab is going to say that glove right there made this mark right here. You've nearly worn a hole in the forefinger, see? And look, you can make out that hole right here on the chair leg, where this fingerprint powder shows the glove marks."

"Anybody could have been wearing the gloves," he protested, watching me smooth fingerprint tape over the black powder.

"And put them back in your jacket pocket in your bedroom closet while you were asleep? Come on, Olead." I lifted the glove mark, taped it down on an index card, and carefully labeled it. I put the gloves in a plastic bag, stapled the bag shut, and labeled it. I stopped and wrote in my notebook. That was when Olead asked me what I was doing, and he made that adolescent wisecrack about the crime scene.

After his attempt at humor, he sat back down on the hall floor, cross-legged, and watched me. I struggled to turn the chair right side up and get it back out in the hall, out of the way. "You want me to help you with that?" Olead asked.

"No," I told him, but he already had caught hold of the

other arm of the chair and was tugging it into the hall. We got it set down, and I said, "Thanks," because I didn't know what else to say.

He watched me a while longer, watched me lift a few more glove marks, and then he said, "Deb, if you find a bag of marbles in there, they're mine."

I straightened. "What?" I asked incredulously.

"A bag of marbles," he said, fairly casually. "It's a blue velveteen bag, one of the kind Seagram's Crown Royal comes in, and it's got about twenty or twenty-five marbles in it, and they're mine, and I want them."

"Why?" I asked.

His mouth took on that mulish look familiar to most parents of fifteen-year-olds, boys or girls, and he said, "They're mine and I want them because they're mine."

"I'll see about it if I find them," I said and lifted a chest of drawers that was lying face down. It was surprisingly light, mainly because the drawers weren't in it. As I scooted it to the side I heard Olead's quick indrawn breath, and I looked down.

We had found Brenda.

3

Olead had told me Brenda was four years old. I thought she must be close to five. She was lying in the position of sleep, face down on a faded blue sleeping bag that was zipped to her waist. Her head, on a blue pillowcase, was turned to the left side so that she was facing away from the door of the room, toward the wall at the front of the house. She was a thin child, small-boned, with straight dark-blonde hair. Her little hands were open and relaxed, and a small pink plush squirrel had fallen away from one of them.

You could have put your fist through the hole in her back. Even if you were Captain Millner's size.

The person who shot her had not done it from close range, and a shot pattern spreads more and more the farther away it gets from the muzzle of the shotgun.

Olead had risen to his feet. "No," he said under his breath, "no, no, no—" He approached her, squatted down on the floor, touched her hair with his big hand. He looked up at me with a completely adult grief in his eyes and he said, "You think I did that. You think I did that to Brenda."

I didn't answer. I just looked at him.

"No," he said, "no, I didn't, but I can promise you this, you won't keep me in any jail or nuthouse you try to put me in, because I'm going to find out who did that to Brenda and when I find him he's going to pay for it."

I stepped out into the hall. "Captain Millner," I called, "I think Olead is ready to go to jail now."

Millner came in, walking fast, and stopped short at the sight of the man crouching over the body of the child. "So you found her," he said.

Olead looked up. "You promised me I could stay until we find Jeffrey," he said, his voice thick with tears. "I promise I'll go quietly then. But if anybody tries to take me now they're going to have to fight me. I want to find Jeffrey. Jeffrey's alive. Nobody would kill Jeffrey; he's only a baby."

For a moment I had glimpsed the man that must be somewhere inside of him. But now he was a child again, begging the grown-ups to put his broken world back together for him.

"Brenda's a baby, too," I said, hearing my voice come out almost as a monotone.

"But you don't understand," he said earnestly. "Brenda's old enough to talk. She—maybe she saw something. Maybe she saw who did it. But Jeffrey—even if Jeffrey saw he's not old enough to tell. Nobody would have any reason to kill Jeffrey."

"Brenda was asleep," I said. "You can tell that from the way she's lying. She didn't see anything. That wasn't why she was killed."

"No, you don't understand," Olead said again. "Maybe —maybe somebody thought she saw something. Nobody would kill Jeffrey. He's only fifteen months old. Nobody— nobody—nobody would kill Jeffrey."

"Whoever killed Brenda would kill Jeffrey," Captain Millner said harshly. "Get your pictures, Deb." He turned away, adding over his shoulder, "Sit down, Olead. I said you could stay and you can, as long as you keep out of the way. But you get your ass over here in the hall and sit down."

Olead went back in the hall and sat down on the floor, and Captain Millner headed toward the living room. That's one of the better facets of Captain Millner: he leaves people alone to do their work.

I took photographs of the body. I made measurements and recorded them in my notebook, so that I would be able to describe, later, exactly how the body had been lying when it was found. And then I let the people from the Medical Examiner's transport crew, who had been called out to get the bodies from the den, take this one too.

Olead got out of the way to let them into the room.

They didn't move this small body on a gurney. They just gathered her up, sleeping bag and pillow and all, and zipped her into a black plastic body bag. Olead watched them do it, his face completely impassive. One of the attendants looked at him, his eyes expressive of utter contempt, and Olead stared back at him. Then, as they went out through the living room with their burden, he sat back down on the floor.

I glanced at my watch. It was only 5:00 A.M. It felt as if it ought to be ten or eleven o'clock.

I stepped around the blood on the floor and tried to move a second chest of drawers. It slipped from my hands and crashed to the floor, and Bob, in the den, called, "Deb?"

"I'm okay," I shouted back. "Just dropped something."

Olead was on his feet. "Shut up!" he shouted. "Damn you, shut up!" Bob and Shea and Captain Millner all headed toward us, Shea with his hand on his pistol again. Olead was still momentarily, his head cocked to the side, listening, and suddenly he dived past me to start grabbing at furniture.

Shea caught him by the shoulders to try to pull him back, and he bucked Shea off and pitched a full dresser drawer across the room. Millner yelled, "Back off, Shea!"

Because this time we all heard it, a faint whimper from the far left corner of the room, the area that seemed the core of the chaos. Olead tore at the pile of furniture, and Millner and Bob Castle waded into it too, handing things back to Shea in the hall, as the whimper grew into a wail.

I could hear Olead panting, his breath coming out almost in sobs, and with every breath, he was saying, "Jeffrey—Jeffrey—Jeffrey—"

And then he was under the overturned mattress of a king-size bed, and he stood up, balancing the weight of that and the double set of box springs and a big chair on his shoulders like Samson in the wreckage of the Philistine temple, and he panted, "Deb, get him, get him—"

The space he had made was barely large enough for me to crawl through, even though I crouched over as low as I could. The crib was crushed, but the bars had folded over the mattress, and the baby apparently had gone right on sleeping on the mattress on the floor. I snatched him up and backed out, and Olead came out and let the furniture crash back to the floor. The sound was still echoing when he grabbed the crying baby from my arms and stood holding him.

Shea reached for him again and Millner caught his arm. "No," he said, "let him be."

Olead now seemed totally oblivious to everybody and everything else, as he crooned to the baby in his arms. "Oh, you're wet," he said. "Jeffrey, you're worse than wet, and I can't get at your diapers, now what am I going to put on you, huh, kid? What am I going to do with you?" His voice broke, as he repeated, "Oh, God, Jeffrey, what am I going to do with you?"

Millner reached in his pocket and thrust a five-dollar bill at Shea. "Find a store," he said. "Get some Pampers or something."

I wasn't sure Olead had heard. He crossed the hall toward the bathroom, talking steadily to the baby, and I followed him and watched as he began to run the bathtub full of water. I glanced at Millner, and he nodded. "Somebody's got to do it," he pointed out. It was definitely true that Jeffrey was worse than wet. "Just stay with them," he added.

I sat in the bathroom, on the only available seat, and watched Olead as he knelt on the bathmat, bathing the baby with as much absorption as if it were a perfectly normal day. Without taking his eyes off Jeffrey, he got a plastic duck out of the shelf under the sink; it was followed by a green sponge in the shape of a fish. Olead said, "Fishie's gonna git you," and the baby chortled and splashed. Olead, said, "Fishie's gonna bite your ears clean—Fishie's gonna splash your hair—oh! That was a big splash the duck made!" He wiped some of the water off his face and chest.

"Spash," the baby said gleefully, and Olead lifted him out of the tub and wrapped him in a towel and opened the drain.

Shea, looking exasperated, was back with the diapers, and Olead thanked him distantly and went on talking to the baby. "You gonna have to get by without powder, sport, because I don't know where your powder is." He diapered the baby and said, "It's too early for you to be up." He went to the kitchen, walking through the den without a glance at the evidence techs still working, or at the blood and the chalk marks. He opened the refrigerator, got out a carton of milk. He poured some of it in a glass cup, put it in the microwave and set the timer for half a minute, and then, expertly juggling baby, bottle, and cup, he poured the warm milk into a plastic bottle and put a screw-on nipple on it.

Then he looked puzzled.

His face cleared, and he walked into the living room, where Shea had parked himself on the couch. Very politely, he said, "Would you get up, please?"

Shea looked at him.

"Would you get up, please?" Olead asked again, not quite so politely and a little more loudly.

Shea went on looking at him.

"Shea," Millner said.

Shea got up, and Olead tried, with one hand and his hip, to move the couch. Millner realized what he was doing and went to help. "Shea," he said, and Shea, with a very disgusted look on his face, joined in the effort.

The two couches, pushed together, made a safe if rather

large crib. Olead laid the baby down and offered him the bottle; the baby took it, but as soon as Olead turned his back, the baby began to wail. I could make out a repeated cry of "Oyee! Oyee!"

Olead looked at Millner. Millner shrugged, and Olead climbed over the arm of the couch and lay down beside the baby. The wailing stopped.

"What the—" Shea began disgustedly.

"Shut up," Millner said.

"But are you going to just let him—"

"Shut up, Shea," Millner repeated. "That baby doesn't know what's happened. We've called welfare and somebody's on the way over to get the kid. But until she gets here, the kid gets what he wants, and if what he wants is big brother, he gets big brother. Hear me?"

"But that crazy bastard could—"

"Shut up, Shea," Millner repeated a third time. "Deb, stay in here."

Five minutes later, Olead climbed back over the arm of the couch. "He's asleep," he said. "He doesn't usually get up till about seven-thirty. I think it was that crash that woke him up so early." He looked at me. "Will those people from welfare take care of him?" he asked.

"They'll take care of him."

"Can I stay till they get here?"

"You just wanted to stay till he was found," Millner reminded him.

"Yeah, but—but—he's allergic to some stuff," Olead said. "I need to tell them."

Millner shrugged. "You've stayed this long, yeah, you might as well go on staying."

Olead followed me back to the bedroom and asked again, "Can I help you move some of that stuff?"

"I don't need to move any more of it right now," I said. I had found the ejected shell from the round that had killed Brenda. It was a very old one, red paper. The ones in the den had been plastic. I had no reason to expect to find anything else evidentiary in there. I would have to finish the room, of course, but I would wait until Olead was gone.

"Then can I move stuff?" he asked.

"I'd rather you wouldn't," I told him. "We'll do it later."

"But I've got to find my marbles!" he protested frantically.

I looked at Millner. Millner said, "I don't want you in there, Olead. We'll look for your marbles later."

"It's important," he protested.

"They'll turn up," I assured him.

Behind him, Shea waved his hand in a circular motion around his head, in a gesture that had always meant "flaky," and I nodded. And yet it was strange, he'd seemed completely normal while he was caring for the baby. Whatever was wrong with him, it seemed to come and go.

Olead turned, his hands in his pockets. "Then can I start cleaning the den?" he asked. "I don't like blood all over the floor." He headed that way.

"No, you can't start cleaning the den," Millner said behind him, beginning to sound exasperated.

"But—"

"We aren't through with it," I told him.

He looked at the chalk marks. "Oh," he said. "Then is it okay if I wash the dishes?"

"Yes, for crying out loud, wash the dishes," Millner told him, and Olead gathered up the plates from the dining room as Millner added to me, "Stay with him."

"Could I help you with that?" I asked Olead.

He looked down at the plates in his hands. "No, I—I kind of think I've got to be doing something." He unplugged the coffeepot and poured the stale coffee down the drain. "Besides," he added, "Mother would have a fit if she knew the house was full of people with the kitchen looking like this."

"My kitchen is almost always about ten times worse than this," I told him as he stacked the silver.

He glanced at me. "But that's different," he told me. "You have other things to think about than how the house looks. Mother doesn't—didn't. It's hard to remember to say that," he said. "Past tense, I mean. That's hard to remember. Is it okay for me to take my vitamins?"

I told him it was okay to take his vitamins.

"Good," he said. "The doctor says I have to take them every day."

By the time the woman from welfare arrived, the kitchen was clean. Olead looked her over doubtfully and announced, "He's allergic to scented baby powder."

"So many babies are," she answered. "I always use cornstarch."

"Well, yeah, and—and he doesn't like eggs."

"He has to have eggs, unless he's allergic to them."

"He's not. And the doctor says he has to have them so he won't get anemic. But he doesn't like them. You have to kind of sneak them in disguised. Oh, and he can't have chocolate. It upsets him."

"I'll take good care of him," she assured Olead, with a gentleness that suggested to me somebody outside had told her Olead's condition. "What doctor does he go to? I'll need to get a copy of his shot record."

Jeffrey, awakened when she lifted him, wailed again for Oyee and thrust out his arms. Olead took him and said, "Jeffrey, you have to go with this lady. She's going to take good care of you. I can't keep you, Jeffrey; you wouldn't like where I'm going." He put him back in the woman's arms and very gently pried loose the little fingers that were frantically clinging to him. "He doesn't like strangers," he explained unsteadily. "He's a good baby, though. Really, he's a good baby."

"I'm sure he's a good baby," she agreed. "None of them like strangers at this age. But I won't be a stranger long. He'll be okay, I promise." Expertly, she dressed him in a yellow knit romper suit she took out of her purse.

"Yeah," Olead said, and watched as she went out the

door with the baby bundled up in a blanket she had brought with her.

Then he pulled the couches apart at one end and sat down on one, and wept. It must have been five minutes before he stopped. We all just let him cry. There was no doubt that he needed to cry.

After he was silent again, Captain Millner said, "Olead, you've got to go to the jail now. You promised not to fight."

"Yeah, but does Shea have to take me?"

"Yes, he does," Millner said with quiet finality.

Olead stood up and wiped his face with the back of his hands. "I guess you want to put handcuffs on me," he said.

"You better believe it," Shea told him harshly.

Olead turned his back and put his hands behind him. "This way?" he asked.

I thought Shea was at least mildly disappointed that Olead hadn't tried to fight. But he put the handcuffs on him, led him out to the police car, tucked him into the caged back of it, and drove away.

"He doesn't know he did it," I said. "He honestly doesn't know it. If you ran him on a polygraph he'd come out looking innocent."

"No doubt about that," Millner agreed. "Damn, even after all I've seen here I can't help feeling sorry for him. There was something screwy in this family, Deb, something besides him. Did you notice that baby never once cried for his mother? He just kept calling for Olead."

"I noticed," I said. "I'm going to go back into that room and search it completely. I want to know why he wanted that marble bag so much. I wonder if there's something *in* it."

"I'd like to know that myself," Millner agreed. "I'm going to look through the desk. We need to find some family."

It was midafternoon before I parked in my own driveway. My front door opens onto a very short entry hall which seems like part of the living room. Inside, my own family was cocooned in a comfortable mess of newspapers, magazines, popcorn, and the televised football game. Harry, who on business days is a very precision-minded test pilot for Bell Helicopter, hadn't shaved. As he also hadn't shaved the two previous days, he looked distinctly scruffy, an appearance somewhat enhanced by his old Marine utility pants (he hasn't been a Marine in sixteen years), his paint-spattered T-shirt, and the large hole in his left sock, which was one of a pair of socks I had thrown away three times. He keeps rescuing them. Becky, who is nineteen and has her first full-time job, was reading the Sears catalog, and Hal, who is the reason I know so much about fifteen-year-old boys, was playing Pac-Man on his watch.

Of course, I asked if Vicky had gone to the hospital, and of course, Harry said no and reminded me she wasn't supposed to go yet. I didn't believe that. Look, Vicky had gained sixty-eight pounds, and *nobody* gains sixty-eight pounds in just seven months.

Anyway, I would like to see that baby sometime soon. I started to work when Hal was only six months old because Harry was in school and his VA check didn't quite stretch to fit all our needs. I picked the police department almost by chance, because they were advertising when I needed work, and although the pay isn't that good for the men, it is—or was then, anyway—more than most women were getting. I've liked being a cop, and the situation clearly hasn't hurt the kids—Hal brags about me a lot—but I had missed having the time with him I had with the girls. I sort of felt I was a baby short, in playing time. And Vicky had promised to let me baby-sit.

By the time that thought had crossed my mind, Becky looked up and grunted a sort of greeting. Hal, not looking up, shouted delightedly, "Hey, Mom, I got up to nine hundred and ten!" His watch made musical noises and he yelled, "Watch me get that monster! Oh, darn." He put the watch down. "Hey, Mom, you want some popcorn?"

"No," I said, "I think I want to throw up."

Harry shook the newspaper and the cat off his lap and followed me into the bedroom, where I had curled into a tight little knot of misery with all my clothes on. He started to rub my back. "Who owns the problem?" he asked me. We were reading self-help books last year.

"Me, right now," I answered.

"Is it the Baker boy?" he asked. "Is that the case you're on?"

"Uh-huh," I said. "Is it already on TV?"

"Yeah. I knew his daddy. Real nice fellow. Creamed his private plane into the side of a mountain in New Mexico in a thunderstorm about five years back. You want to talk about the case?"

"I know he did it, but I don't want him to have done it," I said, realizing I was doing just what I sometimes accuse the kids of doing, trying to live in the world as I wanted it to be rather than in the world as it is.

Harry went on rubbing my back. "You know," he said presently, "I've known your head to be wrong about a lot of things, but I don't think I've ever known your heart to guess wrong."

"But all the evidence—"

"Maybe you better start asking how it could have been faked."

"But if he didn't do it, who did?"

"Lady, there's one detective in this family, and it sure as hell ain't me." He went on rubbing my back, and after a while I went to sleep, waking hours later when Becky had detached herself from the Sears catalog long enough to go out to Ron's and get some fried chicken. I had chicken and beer for supper, and afterwards I asked Hal to stop playing Pac-Man in the living room.

Thirty minutes later I asked Hal to turn off the sound effects if he insisted on playing Pac-Man in the living room. The musical notes stopped abruptly, but the verbal accompaniment went on.

Becky was now reading the Ward's catalog.

Harry brought me another beer. Channel ten was showing a rerun of parts of the Rose Parade, and I watched half-heartedly.

Becky reached for the Penney's catalog and said persuasively, "Mom, if I got a *raise* would you let me have my own credit card?"

"Ask the store for a credit card," I told her. "Don't ask me."

Hal groaned and said, "A ghost ate me." Becky stared at him, and he said, "On my *watch*. My *Pac-Man* watch. You know, a ghost? The little man who was not there?"

Somebody who wasn't there—Olead said he didn't eat breakfast. We all assumed that he was lying, or that he didn't remember. But maybe he wasn't lying and maybe he did remember. If he didn't eat breakfast, then just who was the fifth plate for? A man at the party, a man who said he might like to go hunting too—three shotguns, three shotguns in the house, maybe three men who were going hunting? Only one of them had something else in mind?

If Olead didn't eat breakfast—if there was some way to prove whether Olead had eaten breakfast—

He threw up that morning and Shea flushed it, the blithering idiot—besides, that could also have told us—

A urinalysis; maybe it wasn't too late for us to catch part of the proof that Olead might not be lying.

I reached for my car keys. "I've got to go to the jail," I said. "I just thought of something."

Harry looked startled. "You've had two beers," he pointed out. "Can't you just call the jail?"

Reluctantly, I put down my car keys. "I guess," I said. "But I'm afraid he won't cooperate."

"He who? And why wouldn't he?"

"Olead. I'm afraid he won't see a reason for it."

Harry looked as if he wanted to ask what I was talking about; then he shrugged and handed me the phone, and I called the jail.

Olead didn't want to cooperate. He couldn't see what I

wanted to find out with a urinalysis. I had to talk to him on the phone, finally, and then I talked to an evidence tech, who told me it had to go to the lab in Austin and it would probably take about three weeks. I asked why it couldn't just go to the lab in Garland, and she said, "Well, because they won't do it, mainly. They'd just turn around and send it to the lab in Austin, and that'd take—"

"Another week. I know. Okay. Fine. So send it to Austin."

I hung up.

Damn Shea. Damn that stupid idiot bastard, hadn't he ever been to any kind of school on crime scene search and preservation of evidence?

Damn Shea.

Damn Shea.

Harry brought me another beer and, of course, I threw up.

Shea was well past any respect for my age, rank, sex, or any other such infirmity. It was nine o'clock the morning of January second, and he'd gone on duty at eleven o'clock the night before, after a somewhat exhausting previous night. He didn't appreciate my questions; now he shouted, "What the hell do you mean what did it look like? It looked like *puke!*"

"Okay," I shouted, "did it look like egg and bacon and grits and toast puke, or did it look like creamed tuna on waffles with green peas puke?" I happen to despise that word. But I was about to the point of despising Shea more.

"How the hell do I know?" he shouted. "I don't go around sticking my head in the john! It looked like puke!" He muttered something else under his breath. It sounded like "bitch."

"*Officer* Shea," I said as sweetly as I could manage, "you shut your foul mouth and you try listening for a change. We have a murder suspect, right? And he denies eating breakfast, right? Only there were five plates. And there's just an outside chance he might be telling the truth, and if he didn't eat breakfast somebody else did. And if somebody else was in that house eating breakfast at two or two-thirty A.M. then somebody else could have shot those five people. On top of that, the suspect denies hearing five shotgun blasts. He may be lying. But if he is telling the truth, the only way he could have not heard five shotgun blasts that close to him was if he was heavily drugged. Well, did you notice he was acting a little dopey? And did he happen to mention to you, as he did to me, that he felt like he'd had an overdose? He really doesn't think he was drugged, but it's a possibility. Now, you were in a position to be able to ascertain whether the suspect ate breakfast and whether the suspect was drugged. Only you didn't see fit to preserve the evidence. Officer Shea, I hope you like walking the stockyards at four A.M., because that's where you're going to be for the next few months, if I have anything to say about it."

He pulled off his badge and threw it down on the desk and said, "Like hell I am!"

I asked for his ID card too, fast before he had time to change his mind.

He said "bitch" a few more times and said he was sorry he wasn't a pretty boy like Olead Baker, and then he stomped out.

Captain Millner managed not to laugh until Shea got on the elevator. I thought that was decent of him. But before the door slid closed, somebody looked out of forgery and asked, "Did he get on the elevator that has the bullet hole in it?"

I said he did, and the person in forgery—I didn't see who it was—said, "Good, I'd hate to have both elevators messed up."

The door closed on a new burst of profanity, and Captain Millner shook his head. "Worst case of rookie-itis I've seen in quite a while," he pronounced, and added, "Deb, you want to tell me what you've got?"

"A mare's-nest, I'm afraid," I answered. "But I need to go back out to that house again."

"Finish up your paperwork and I'll go with you," he said. He glanced at the elevator. "I wonder how long it's going to take Shea to figure out that you don't have any say-so about his assignments."

"I hope it doesn't take too long," I said. "I don't want to sit here and wait for him all day long." I looked at the badge and ID card on my desk. "What I yelled at him about isn't really what I'm the maddest at him about anyway."

Millner chuckled. "I didn't think it was," he said. He sat down in another chair in our little office, which happens to have been originally designed as an interrogation room. The four desks and chairs crammed into it now have made it rather claustrophobic, especially in view of the fact that there are six people in the squad. "I didn't really think it was," he repeated and began to read the report from the evidence technicians. He looked up. "Deb," he said, "I'd like it to be somebody else too. But I don't care what else you explain away, we're stuck with a bruise on his shoulder, and that bruise was made by the butt of a twelve-gauge shotgun."

"I know it," I said. "I know it, blast it, and I've got to figure out where he got it."

"And we were just as much at fault as Shea," Millner added. "More, maybe, because he's a rookie, and we ought to know better."

"Better than what?"

"Think about it," Millner said. "Suppose he *was* telling the truth. Suppose there was another person there. Suppose Olead went on sleeping and somebody else ate breakfast. Where would he have left his fingerprints? On the coffee cup. And where's the coffee cup?" He answered his own question. "We—*I*—let Olead Baker wash it. That's where the coffee cup is."

4

Captain Millner was still in my office when Shea came back in looking sheepish. "Can I have my badge and ID back?" he asked.

"Sit down, Shea," Millner said.

Shea sat.

"Nobody likes puke," Millner told him. "But in this sort of an investigation, absolutely anything at all can turn out to be evidence. Did you ever hear about a very important case up north in which a major piece of evidence was two cigarette butts floating in the toilet? That is, they would have been an important piece of evidence, until a patrolman went in to take a leak and flushed. The man who was convicted of the murder was the victim's husband. He didn't smoke. Neither did the victim, and the toilet was in an upstairs bathroom off the master bedroom. The husband was acquitted, on his second trial, after the patrolman finally decided to admit his error. But by then the man had already done six years for murder. He was almost certainly innocent. And he was a doctor, Shea. He'd done a lot of good for a lot of people. He could have been doing a lot more good, those six years he was in prison, and the years after that when he was trying to get his medical license back."

Shea didn't answer. He looked at his hands.

"I know you heard the story, because I told it to your recruit class. Now, Olead Baker's almost surely guilty." Millner glanced at me as if expecting an argument. "But he doesn't know it, Shea. I'd like to be able to prove it to him."

"I'm sorry." Shea was still looking at the table.

"All right, you don't have the corner on screwing up," Millner said. "We all did it. We all walked in, looked at the scene, decided the kid did it, and forgot to use our brains to look at other possible alternatives. But you made another bad mistake."

"What's that?"

"Baker says after he vomited you walked around in his room and then went out and told him to go in there and change clothes. Is that about accurate?"

"Yeah," Shea admitted, "fairly accurate."

"When you were walking around in there, did you look for weapons?" Millner asked casually.

"Of course I did," Shea said indignantly. "That's what I was really doing when he thought I was just walking around."

"Where did you look?" Millner asked, beginning to light a cigarette.

"Well, in the drawers, and on the closet shelf and floors, and under the bed."

"Was the door open or closed?"

"The bedroom door? Well, I guess it was open. Yeah, it had to be, because I was keeping an eye on him at the same time. Why?"

"I thought it might be," Millner said. "That explains why you didn't find the loaded shotgun behind the bedroom door."

"The *what?* You're kidding! You're kidding, aren't you?" he said, his expression oddly similar to that of Olead, a child begging the grown-ups to fix a suddenly unfamiliar world.

"There was a twelve-gauge shotgun behind the bedroom door," I told him. "I found it when I was in there talking to him—or rather, he found it and I took charge of it. I pumped three rounds out of it."

"And what that says, Shea, is that if he did do it, and if he hadn't burned off his fit by the time you got there, he'd have killed you about three o'clock yesterday morning," Millner said precisely. "You gave him the means to do it. Shea, there are two kinds of cops who are dangerous to themselves and other cops. That's cops who don't think and cops who think they're smarter than they are. You're both. Did you call for a backup before you tried to go in?"

"Well, no, I—"

"You had one on the way. I know you did, because they always dispatch a backup for any kind of call, let alone a report of shots fired. Did you wait for the backup to get there?"

"Well, I—"

"Did you wait for your backup to get to the back door and cover it? What would have happened if he had gone out the back door?"

"Well—"

Feeling sick, I asked, "You can't even tell me whether the back door was locked or not, can you?"

"No," he said. "Does it matter?"

"It could matter," Millner said slowly. "Yes, it could matter very much." He slid the badge and ID across the table. "Get out of here, Shea," he said tiredly. "I've seen enough of you for one day."

I still couldn't go to the house again as I wanted to, because the DA's office had called and said there was a committal hearing set for eleven o'clock and before that they wanted me to come over and sign a warrant. Some brainless wonder of an assistant DA had decided we were going to charge Olead and then let him get off on an insanity plea if he could. It didn't make a whole lot of sense to me.

But whether it made sense to me or not, we were going to have a committal hearing, to decide whether there was just cause to hold him, and to decide whether bail should be set, and then, of course, after the hearing was over, he would be locked back up without bail. But the court had to say so.

What actually followed the hearing was not as obvious as that conclusion was. I still haven't figured out how it happened. A person believed to be a homicidal maniac, a person suspected of the shotgun murders of five people, doesn't just walk out of the courtroom and disappear.

But Olead Baker did.

They were going to put a special bulletin out, have everybody combing the town looking for him, but I said, "Wait a minute. Don't do it yet—there's no need to panic the whole city. I think I know where he went. Let me go look for him. Give me half an hour."

Captain Millner conferred with the sheriff. Then he said unhappily, "Half an hour. No longer."

I left the courtroom. I didn't get in a police car; I just picked up a walkie-talkie, and I walked east on Houston Street to the big telephone company building. Then I turned left and crossed the street at the Convention Center and walked along in front of it until I crossed the street again and headed into the Water Garden. In January, the trees were bare, but the shrubbery is evergreen, and the fountains sprayed into the air and the waterfalls tumbled down their geometrically shaped staircases that narrowed and narrowed all around until the water churned, foaming, into a little central pool scarcely six feet in diameter. There is a little spray-wet observation platform down at the bottom of the waterfalls, just above the surface of the central pool, and a familiar figure was sitting on the observation platform. I said into my walkie-talkie, "I've got him. Everything is all right. I'm going to take him to lunch before I bring him back in."

"Ten-four," Captain Millner said.

It was an unusual thing to do. But this was an unusual case.

I walked down to the stepping stones, onto the observation platform. I sat down beside him. Without turning his head, he said, "Hello, Deb. You didn't need to come looking for me. I'd have come back."

"I know you would," I said untruthfully. "But the sheriff

was rather upset. I thought it would be better if I was with you."

"Yeah, I guess so," he said absently. "I guess I'm an escapee. I didn't mean to be. I just—I just wanted to take a walk."

"It's too chilly down here for me," I said. "Do you mind if we walk back up on top?"

"That's okay," he said indifferently. "I just wanted to see it again, that's all." He headed up the stepping stones, with me behind him. At the top, he sat down on a low concrete wall. "I just wanted to see it again," he repeated. "Where are they going to send me, Deb?"

I told him I didn't know.

"Well, I don't guess it matters much," he said.

"I've got something for you," I told him.

"What's that?" he asked, not sounding very interested.

I opened my purse and took out an embroidered blue velveteen bag. I put it in his hand. He looked down at it. He opened the gold-colored drawstrings and emptied the contents out into his hand. I'd already looked, several times, but I looked again now. Seven solid-color yellow marbles and four solid-color blue ones, small, apparently from a Chinese checker game. Five steel ball-bearings, in two different sizes. Two chipped glass marbles, apparently old ones, and three pretty swirly marbles of the kind we used to call cat's-eyes when I was nine years old.

He poured them back into the bag and pulled the drawstring closed again, and he clenched the bag tightly in his right hand. He bowed his head over it, and his shoulders shook with tearing sobs. He was crying again, and this wasn't a child's sorrow; this was a man's terrible grief I was seeing. His hands clenched and unclenched on the velveteen bag as he struggled to get control of himself.

Then, finally, he half-chuckled through the tears. "I'll bet you wondered why I wanted these, didn't you?"

I admitted the question had crossed my mind.

He looked back down at the bag in his hand. "I want to

try to explain," he said. "To start off, I think my mother shouldn't have ever had children. She wasn't a maternal sort of person. I'm not saying that was what made me schizo, because it wasn't, but it didn't help any. Brenda has just sort of brought herself up, and when I got home six months ago I completely took over the care of Jeffrey and most of the care of Brenda. Well, that may give you some idea of what it was like for me before I went to the hospital, with me being at that time an only child. Mother was determined to do her duty as she saw it. She never abused me, and she never neglected me, but she never loved me. No, maybe I'd better rephrase that. She loved me, but she never liked me. I guess Dad loved me, and I know he liked me, but he was pretty well determined to do his duty, too. Well, Brenda and Jeffrey didn't even know they had a big brother—half-brother—until the doctor said I could go home. Then Mother and Jack informed Brenda—rather stiffly, I'd guess, knowing Mother—that they had a big brother who had been in a sort of hospital, and now he was better and was coming home."

He looked down again at the blue bag, emptied the marbles back out into the palm of his hand. "I'd been living in Fort Worth all that time. But I'd never even seen them before. I guess it was just as well. Anyhow, Brenda went around the neighborhood and told everybody her big brother was coming home. She wanted to get a present for her big brother. Mother said it wasn't necessary. But she *really* wanted to. She asked her friends what kind of a present to get for a big brother. But remember, Brenda was four years old. To her, a big brother was somebody maybe seven or eight years old. And some kid told her a big brother might like a bag of marbles. She went around trying to find one. An older kid in the neighborhood, I think about twelve years old, conned her out of her life savings—four dollars and twenty-two cents, she told me later—for this."

He looked down at her present, rolled the marbles back into the bag. "She was upset when she saw me, realized my age. She was afraid I wouldn't like her present. But she took her courage in both hands and gave it to me anyway, and I promised her I would treasure it forever. The reason it was in that room—she came in a couple of days ago and told me she didn't like sleeping in the room with Aunt Edith and could she borrow my marble bag until Aunt Edith left. She thought it must be some kind of a talisman, because I always kept it on my windowsill, right beside my bed." He glanced at it again. "Well, it was a talisman. Because, Deb, this is the only thing that anybody has ever given me in my entire life that was given just out of love, and for no other reason."

He closed the bag, tied it closed. "Keep it for me, would you, please? I know I can't have it in jail. But I want to know it's being taken care of."

I think, looking back on it, that it must have been then that I really decided he couldn't have done it. Before, I had just been wishing he hadn't done it, or thinking, vaguely, that maybe there was somebody else. But at that moment a hunch and a hope solidified into a certainty, and I began to wonder who had done it and how I could prove it, and whether Olead had been deliberately framed. All thoughts of making him realize he had done it himself were gone.

He stood up. "I'm ready to go back now. I guess walking away like that was pretty stupid, but I'm not a bit sorry I did it. Thank you for bringing this to me." He put the blue bag in my hand.

"I told the captain I was going to take you to lunch before I took you back in," I said. "Where would you like to go?"

He shrugged. "Anywhere. Wherever you want to go. I don't know downtown. That's really nice of you, Deb."

"I always go to Underground Station," I said. "I'm sort of a salad freak. That okay with you?"

"Sure," he said readily. "You won't get in trouble? I don't want you to get in trouble."

"I won't get in trouble," I told him.

The fact that I always eat lunch at the same time and place, when I can, is fairly well known, and I was late for lunch. As I crossed Houston Street, I saw Becky walking around impatiently by the staircase leading down to the restaurant. Of course I thought of Vicky, and I hurried up to ask, "Has Vicky gone to the hospital?"

"Not that I know of," Becky said. "No, I wanted to show you something. Look, Mom, my very own *credit card!*" I wasn't exactly overwhelmed with delight, as she went on talking, "I applied for it simply weeks ago, but I didn't think I'd really get it, and—" She faltered into silence, suddenly realizing I had somebody with me. "Hi," she said.

"Hi," Olead answered. "Can I look at your credit card?" His tone of voice said he was teasing, but not much, and she handed it to him. He examined it gravely. "Very nice," he decided finally, and handed it back to her and they laughed together.

"Becky, this is Olead Baker," I said, almost praying she hadn't read the newspapers or seen the television news. But Becky is not known for keeping up with current events, and she was running true to form.

"Hello, Olead," she said, and he smiled.

"Hi, Becky," he answered, and asked, "Were you going to have lunch with your mother? I was too."

"Good," she said, and as we went down the stairs and got in line for the salad bar, she at once plunged into a complicated tale of backbiting at the secretarial agency that employed her. She finished only after we were seated, exclaiming dramatically, "Now, can you top that?"

Olead, without smiling, answered softly, "Yes, I think I can, but I don't want to right now."

I explained, "Olead has reason to believe he's been framed for murder."

He glanced at me, his expression startled, and then he added, "And I don't want to talk about it now. You can read about it in the newspaper, and your mother can tell you however much isn't in the newspaper, but I don't want to talk about it now. Please, I'd really rather hear about what you're doing."

Becky is never averse to talking. She talked, and she talked, and she talked, and Olead and I put in an occasional word, and then the meal was over. Olead stood up. "Becky," he said, "I have to go to jail now and I don't like it. But there's nothing I can do about it. Will you—let me kiss you? Just for a minute? So I can have that to think about?" He glanced at me. "You don't mind much, do you?" he asked.

I told him I wouldn't see a thing, but of course I did; I saw the gentleness in his expression and I saw a surprised look on Becky's face, and then he said softly, "Thank you, Becky," and he looked over at me. "I'm ready to go," he said.

He didn't talk as we crossed the street to the police station, and I didn't ask him anything. We went to the elevators and got the one with the bullet hole in it and he asked about it and I told him—nothing at all dramatic, just a spot of carelessness—and then I walked with him into my office. "Sit down," I said.

He sat.

"You and I have some thinking to do," I told him. "If you didn't do it, who did?"

"I don't know," he answered. "Don't you think I've tried to figure it out? I can't come up with anything."

"Then let's think some more. The murders look like the work of a homicidal maniac." He winced. I ignored that, and went on, "That means they were either committed by a homicidal maniac, or they were committed by someone who wanted them to look like the work of a homicidal maniac. Olead, what I'm saying is that if you didn't do it then you were deliberately framed, and you were framed by someone who knows enough about your background to be able to do a convincing job of framing you. And it was done by someone who had a reason for wanting one—or all four—of the adults out of the way."

"And me," Olead answered quietly.

"Huh?" I said. I'd been assuming Olead had been

framed just because he was convenient. Who better is there to blame a murder on than a known schizophrenic?

"And me," Olead repeated. "Deb, don't you understand yet? Unless you can find out who really did it, he's murdered me just as surely as he did my mother and sister and the others, except that there's enough of me left alive to know it. Deb, I'm twenty-six years old, and—and—I've never held a job, or driven a car, or—or—Deb, today was the first time I ever even so much as kissed a girl, do you know that?"

He was shaking. He took a deep breath. "If they get me into prison, or into a hospital for the criminally insane, I'll never get out. Maybe it seems selfish for me to be worrying so much about *me*, when Mother, and Brenda—but Deb, they're through hurting. I hurt, Deb; I *hurt*. I've been shut out of all the important parts of life ever since I was fifteen years old, not by locks and chains—I wasn't locked up much of the time—but shut out by *me*, by a chemical imbalance in my system that made it impossible for me to take part in life. I'm—I was just starting to live, starting to learn how to live."

"Olead," I interrupted, "I understand all that. But you've got to help me. I can't solve it alone. You've got to think now, not just feel."

He took another deep, shuddering breath and visibly forced himself under control. "Okay," he said.

"Who profits, that's one of the first things we ask about any unsolved murder. Olead, who gets your mother's money now?"

"My mother's money?" He stared at me. "My mother didn't have any money."

I frowned. Surely Captain Millner had told me the Bakers had money, and she'd have certainly kept part of it, divorce or no divorce. But maybe I'd misunderstood. "Your stepfather's, then?" One of them had money; that house was money.

"Jack flew a crop-duster," Olead said. "He owned that,

and I guess he had an insurance policy, but that's all. And I guess those'll go to Jeffrey."

"Look," I said, confused, "this doesn't make sense. That's at least a two hundred thousand dollar house up there. *Somebody* had to pay for it."

"Yeah," he agreed, "somebody did. That's my house."

"What?"

"That's my house," he repeated simply. "Mom wanted it, so I bought it, but I bought it in my own name."

"Explain, please," I said.

Looking puzzled by my puzzlement, he said, "I told you my parents were divorced a long time before my father died. At the time of the divorce he changed his will. All his money—I think it wound up being about four million dollars after taxes and all that—came to me. And I told you what he said about keeping things in my name."

All of a sudden this case was looking a whole lot simpler. "Then if you were out of the way, who'd get the money?"

"Well, Jeffrey, of course; he's my only living relative."

"Then who will be Jeffrey's guardian?" Four million dollars, I was thinking. There are a lot of people who'd do murder for four million dollars, four million dollars that would surely escape if a schizophrenic boy became a sane man, a man who would marry, have children.

"The state will have to appoint him one," Olead answered, "because I'm his only living relative."

I felt like I was on a merry-go-round, and it was going faster and faster and I was getting dizzy. "Who—who administers the trust?" I asked.

"What trust?"

"Who takes care of the money for you?"

"It's in the bank. Most of it's in stocks and stuff. There's about three-quarters of a million in money market accounts, and I keep a few hundred thousand liquid."

"Okay, say if it had to be taken out of one bank and put

in another bank, who'd do it? Who was writing the checks to pay for your medical treatment?"

"Me," he answered promptly, and sighed. "Deb, I don't think you know much about what I had."

I had to admit I didn't know much about schizophrenia.

"Well, to start with, there are lots of kinds," he said. "Most are incurable, at least so far as anybody knows right now. What I had—to be honest, I don't even know for sure if it *was* schizophrenia. The old man said it was, Susan says it wasn't, but she wasn't treating me when I was in the acute stage. So at this point all I can really tell you about is what I had and how it acted on me."

"That's all I need to know."

"Well—I say *well* a lot, don't I?"

I agreed that he said *well* a lot, and he said *well* again and then grinned. "It messes up your emotions," he said. "But to a large extent—at least for me—it leaves the brain alone. Well, that's not quite what I mean either, because I had hallucinations, but most of the time I knew they were hallucinations when I was having them. That's scary, in some ways more scary even than when you *don't* know they're hallucinations. And it messes up your verbal thinking, but what it really affects is your emotions. I think I already said that."

"You did."

"Well, then let me put it this way. You're a cop. You're involved in locking me up. You know that and I know that. You do it because it's your job and because I am—quite reasonably—suspected of murder. I didn't do it, but I can see why it's logical for other people to think I did. But if I were schizophrenic now, I would be likely to totally ignore the evidence. I might think you were my enemy. I might think you were putting me in jail so somebody could kill me. I might think you took me to lunch so that a cook at that restaurant could poison me. I might think Becky wasn't really your daughter, she was really a—a CIA agent, or maybe a disguised alien from a supergalactic civilization come to spy on me. Or I might decide that my memories were wrong and I really did kill them and somebody had planted false memories in my head with a thought-ray machine. Or I might think my being arrested had nothing to do with the killings at my house, it was really because I didn't prevent Mount Saint Helens from erupting. See what I'm saying?"

"But you couldn't have prevented Mount Saint Helens from erupting."

"No, but there was a guy at the clinic—still is, for that matter—who thought he could, and he thought it was all his fault. So the rest of us, to cheer him up and try to make him feel better, started telling him, no, it wasn't his fault, it was our fault."

"That sounds mental to me."

"Oh, in a way it is. But remember that at the same time I might be perfectly capable of doing trigonometry and—"

"I was never capable of doing trigonometry in my life," I interrupted, and Olead laughed.

"But what I'm trying to tell you is this," he said. "I wasn't locked in some kind of a barred cell for eleven years. I was in and out. I had bad days, even a few bad weeks to start with, when I flipped out and stayed flipped out, when I had to be locked up. I think I was locked up more than I had to be, but that may be just my opinion. But I was almost all right more time than not. I couldn't function at home and after a while the old man was afraid to let me try to, but I finished high school, at a small private school with some other emotionally disturbed boys, and I went to college, carrying about half of a normal course load per semester, with the college authorities understanding the situation. I have a B.A. from Texas Christian University. And I was at the clinic mainly just because while I was there I couldn't do any damage. Except for letting Mount Saint Helens erupt." He grinned. That apparently was meant to be a joke.

"And I was hospitalized voluntarily," he went on. "I lived at the clinic while I was in high school, and college, and technically I was a patient the whole time. But my father left his entire estate to me unconditionally. Deb, try to understand this. I've never been legally committed to any kind of mental institution. I'm—I was—medically schizophrenic, not legally. I stayed there not because I was being helped, but because I knew when I snapped, when I had the bad times, they'd keep me under control. I was safe there, and other people were safe from me. But meanwhile the doctor was using traditional psychotherapy on me, and it was doing no good at all, and he and I both knew it. I was being kept out of serious trouble. But that was all. Of course," he added thoughtfully, "the fact that he was keeping all my checkbooks locked in his desk drawer did help to keep me there."

"I somehow had it in my head your doctor was a woman."

"The doctor I had died, about eight months ago. I got a different doctor. Susan Braun. I called the old man Dr. Braun, and he didn't do a thing that really helped me. He just kept me doped up so I wasn't too much trouble. Her I call Susan. And she helped me. Helped me," he said. "God. She gave me back my life, that's all."

"Oh?"

"She's interested in orthomolecular therapy. Do you know what that is?"

"Sort of," I said. "It's about vitamins."

"Yeah. It's about vitamins. And she gave me about a thousand times the normal amount of about six different vitamins, and almost overnight, I was well. Oh, I suppose it wasn't quite that fast. I had some pretty wild mood swings there for a while; one day I'd think I was on the top of the heap and the next day I'd feel like the bottom ant in the antbed, but compared to what I had been—" He shook his head. "Deb," he said, "schizophrenia is—or at least a predisposition to it is—genetically transmitted. And that says that in some way nobody understands yet, it is a physical illness. It hurts—physically. I can't exactly explain how, but it does. And the schizophrenic's sweat is different, and his urine is different, and his skin looks different, and his hair looks different. It is a physical illness, more likely several different physical illnesses that all work the same or maybe in tandem. And I had been sick eleven years and I woke up one morning and I was well, almost just like that. The clinic kept me two more months, to get the dosage regulated and to wean me off all the sedatives and other dope I had been on, and they sent me home."

He turned his hands over, looked down at them. "I'm still under psychiatric care for the emotional residue. I have a lot of growing up to do. I have a lot of social adapting to do, because in a lot of ways I'm—as you noticed—emotionally fifteen years old, because that's how old I was when I was effectively yanked out of the world. But that's how I know I'm well now. And that's how I know—know, Deb— that I did not kill anybody at all. I did not kill my sister, or my mother, or my stepfather, or Jake, or Edith. I didn't kill anybody. But whoever killed them would have been a lot kinder to me to have put that shotgun to my head too, even if he did it in a way that made it look like murder-suicide. It wouldn't have mattered if he'd left me to take the blame, if he'd just killed me too."

"Olead, if you were framed we'll find a way to prove it."

"When, Deb?" he asked. "How long is it going to take? My medicine doesn't come in a prescription bottle. You can buy it across the counter, in any health food store and a lot of drugstores and grocery stores. But it doesn't have a prescription number on it. The jail won't let any prisoner have any medicine that's not in a prescription bottle, with a prescription number and 'take as directed' on it. My doctor is on a cruise right now. She's not here to put vitamins in a prescription bottle. And I have to have it every day. *Every* day, Deb. What do you think I'll be like five days from now? I don't want to think about it. And I won't go from here into a private hospital again. I'll go from here to a state hospital. Oh, I won't go to prison, Deb, because by the time I come up for trial an insanity plea won't be a lie. But state hospitals don't tend to experiment with new forms of medication. So when I go there I'll never come out. Now do you understand why I wanted to see the Water Garden just one more time?"

5

"Your degree," I said. "What was it in?"

He looked puzzled. "What does that have to do with anything?"

"Nothing," I answered. "I was just curious."

He shrugged. "It was in psychology." I suppose I must have looked startled, because he chuckled. "Look," he said, "if your head was as messed up as mine was, you'd do anything you could think of to find out why. I minored in biology. I'd give my eyeteeth to get into medical school, but I know that's out. That would have been out even if this hadn't happened."

"Why?"

"Well, because orthomolecular therapy doesn't work on everybody and I suppose there's always the possibility it might stop working for me. Susan says it won't and for me to stop worrying—she even says I may not even need the vitamins that much—but I'm trying to be realistic. If the ailment crept up on me slowly, I might not notice what was happening. Or I could flip out, like I did when I was fifteen. If that happened while I was with a patient—" He shrugged expressively. "*I* wouldn't let me into medical school. So I'm not going to apply. But I can go on and get a doctorate in psychology and work in a clinic, in controlled surroundings, with doctors." He looked down at his hands. "I mean I could have."

"Olead, for heaven's sake don't give up now," I told him. He looked back up at me, startled again, and I thought fast. "Olead," I said, "do you know where Jack kept his shotgun shells?"

"Yeah," he said, "they're—"

"No, don't tell me," I interrupted quickly. "Tell me you're going to show me."

"What are we doing, playing games?"

"If you want to call it that. Look, by law, I can't take out of that house anything that doesn't have a direct bearing on this case. But *you* can; it's your house. So if you told me you refuse to tell me where the shotgun shells are, but if I take you out there you'll show me, and then while we're out there you just happen to take some medicine bottles out of wherever they are and put them in my purse, and then if I wanted to visit you in jail a few minutes every day—"

"Deb," he interrupted, "are you going to get in trouble over this?"

I shrugged. "I could. But that's my concern. I don't think I will."

"I don't want to risk you getting into trouble."

"Olead," I said, "there's something about me that *you* need to understand. Sure, I'm a cop. I've been a cop fifteen years. But I've been a mother a lot longer than that. You're not the first kid in jail I've taken stuff to. Comic books, for a seventeen-year-old rapist. Cigarette money, for an eighteen-year-old prostitute. That sort of thing. The system's not going to collapse because I remember I'm a human being. And the way I see it, your medicine is a lot more important than comic books or cigarette money. Now, I'm asking you again. Do you know where your stepfather kept his shotgun shells?"

"Yeah," Olead said.

"Well, where?"

He looked at me. His eyes dancing, he drawled, "Well, I don't think I want to tell you. But if you'll take me out there I'll be glad to show you."

The police seal was still on the door when we arrived thirty minutes later; we hadn't released the crime scene yet. I opened the door with the key Bob Castle had taken from Jack Carson's pocket, and went in.

The shotgun shells were in a corner of a closet shelf. There were three boxes of them. Two boxes, labeled Federal, contained red plastic shells, and one box, also labeled Federal, contained purple plastic shells. I could not remember seeing purple plastic shotgun shells before, and I was a little puzzled until I remembered they were now color-coded by size by most manufacturers. The purples were 10-gauge, of course. But I was more puzzled by something else.

The empty shotgun shell I picked up off the floor in the room where Brenda was killed was a red paper Winchester, and it had to be around twenty years old, because it's been about that long since anybody made paper shotgun shells. And I could not find any paper shotgun shells in the house, or even any Winchester shells, for that matter. Carson evidently preferred Federal.

"Did he keep any others somewhere else?" I asked Olead.

He shrugged. "Not that I know of. There might have been some in the camper; I don't know."

We went out to the back yard, through the patio and around the pool and to the back of the garage. The camper was not really a camper; it was a camper shell, mounted on the back of a blue Ford pickup truck. The door wasn't locked, and we climbed inside.

There were sleeping bags there, tied up in canvas, and fishing gear that appeared, from its layer of dust, normally to be stored there. There was a tent, also covered with dust. There were cardboard boxes and metal and plastic cases of various types.

I got back out of the truck.

"What's wrong?" Olead asked.

"This isn't really part of the crime scene," I said. "I don't have any business in here."

"But you've got to—"

"I know I've got to. Settle down, kid, we aren't through yet." I got on my radio and asked dispatch to send me a two-man unit. "What's that for?" Olead asked.

"You'll see," I told him.

I got my briefcase out of the car and opened it. "This," I told him, "is a consent-to-search form. When those officers get here to witness it, I want you to sign it. Then we're getting back in that truck."

It took a little while to get us a two-man unit. It was forty-five minutes before we were back in the truck, so that I could begin going through boxes, cases. I found boxes of rifle ammunition, and I found a twenty-two and a thirty-ought-six wrapped in blankets in the bed of the truck. I found pistol ammunition, but no pistol, and I wondered what Jack Carson was doing with three boxes of .45 bullets in the back of his truck.

Especially with nothing to fire it out of.

I didn't find any shotgun shells, red paper or any other color or composition, Winchester or any other brand.

But I did notice that there were three sleeping bags, not two, in the back of the truck, and only one of the three was dusty.

I was beginning to think that this killer was careless. He had expected us to see Olead and not look any farther. But we almost didn't look any farther. If Olead hadn't asked for his marbles—if I hadn't found them—

I went back in the house, Olead tagging after me, and asked, "That night, when you threw up, did you make it all the way to the toilet?"

He looked embarrassed. "Well, almost. Why?"

"Did you hit the bathroom carpet at all?"

"Yeah, some, I think. Shea had delayed me, and I was pretty sick."

"Show me where."

He walked into the bathroom, pointed with the toe of his boot. "There," he said. The carpet, fluffy yellow everywhere else, was discolored in that one spot, and the odor was enough to tell me what had caused the discoloration.

I went and got my pocketknife out of my purse and started cutting out the section of carpet. "What are you doing that for?" Olead asked, watching me intently.

"Laboratory analysis," I answered. "Why would you be sleeping so soundly you would fail to hear four shotgun blasts in the room next to you, and one in the room across the hall? That doesn't make sense."

"It doesn't to me either," he said, "but I'm telling you the truth."

"I didn't say you weren't," I said mildly. "I just want to know why."

"And so do I," he agreed. "But what does that piece of rug have to do with it?"

"You're being dense, Olead," I told him. "You could have been drugged. A chemical analysis of the vomitus might confirm that."

"You told me that yesterday, about the urine sample," he objected, "and I told you then that nobody had a chance to drug me."

"Maybe not," I said, "but I want to know for sure." I put away the pocketknife and put the carpet sample in a plastic bag and stapled it shut. "And now," I told him, "I have to take you back to the jail. Have you taken care of what we came out here for?"

"Yes," he said, "but I can't get your purse closed. There's too many bottles."

"I'll take care of closing my purse," I said, "but you'd better write down for me how many you need of what. Anything I take into the jail has to fit in my pocket, and I don't think I can manage to smuggle in five or six bottles every day."

He went and found a pad and pencil and wrote things down. Tearing that sheet off, he handed it to me and asked, in a slightly too casual tone, "Would you mind if I called Becky sometimes?"

"No, I wouldn't mind," I said, and gave him the telephone number. That piece of paper went in his pocket.

"Can I take something with me to read?" he asked. "I didn't think of that last night, but today when you said comic books—"

"Sure," I told him, "anything within reason." I didn't expect him to choose comic books.

I followed him into his bedroom, where he dithered for a few minutes over whether to take his obviously treasured *Eden Express* with him to jail. That was a book I had read myself, years ago, and I'd been curious enough to do some follow-up reading, with the result that I knew something about it that I had a hunch Olead didn't know. He finally decided against that book, winding up instead with a couple of paperback mysteries and a fat psychology textbook he dug out of a box in the closet.

He paused in the hall. "I suppose you wouldn't let me clean the floor in the den yet."

"I suppose not," I told him. "Olead, it won't do any good to stall. I've got to get in and get some more work done, and there's no way I can keep you out of jail right now."

He shrugged. "Okay," he said. "But there's one more thing I want to show you." He led me back to his room and got a photograph out of a brown envelope in a desk drawer. "That's me," he said, "seven years ago." He put it in my hands.

I would not have recognized him. There was that much difference. He was younger, of course, but age was not the real change. And the real change was not just in his eyes and his expression, although that was most obvious; it was also in his hair, his face, his posture. I would not have turned my back on the man he was then, much less given him access to my purse containing ammunition, handcuffs, and the keys to the detective car I was driving. "I see," I said inadequately.

He put the picture back into the drawer and closed the drawer. "I thought you would," he said. "There aren't any more recent ones. There hasn't been any reason for any. But almost certainly that's what I'll be again, if the medication stops."

I took him back to the jail. On the way in I commented casually, "You like that book *Eden Express?*"

"Yeah, a lot," he said. "It's an autobiography. I don't guess you knew that."

"I've read it. Do you know the man who wrote it is a doctor now?"

"Yeah?" Olead drawled, his eyes alight and his voice amazed. "But he was—Deb, he was as flaky as me."

"I know. And he got over it."

After a moment of silence, Olead asked, in an elaborately casual voice, "Is he a shrink?"

"I think so. I'm not sure."

He sat silently on his side of the car, digesting that piece of information, until I got him out and signed him back into the jail. He apologized to the deputy he had walked away from, and that deputy answered, "Don't ever try it again."

"I won't," Olead assured him.

The deputy patted his holster. "You better not."

"I won't," Olead said again. He tried not to grin. The attempt was not too successful, and the deputy was at a slow simmer as he returned Olead to his cell.

I returned to my office wishing I didn't have to leave Olead there, a feeling I had certainly never had about any other prisoner. I made up my lab request for the carpet fragment, asking for priority treatment for it, and sent it down to ident, so that they could send it off with the other laboratory samples. Then I went to Captain Millner's office.

"Tell me about it," he said.

I told him about it.

"You're making out a pretty good case for the defense," he drawled, "but Deb, you still haven't explained the bruise on his shoulder."

Can you believe it? I had totally forgotten the bruise on his shoulder.

In fifteen years of policing, one thing I've learned and learned well is not to take the job home with me. But this time was going to be different, I realized again, as I got home an hour and a half late to find Becky crying over the newspapers. When she saw me she sniffed a couple of times, folded the newspapers, and looked at me reproachfully.

I looked at the newspapers. She had managed to acquire both the morning and afternoon *Fort Worth Star-Telegram* and both major Dallas papers, as well as assorted smaller papers. "Becky," I asked, "don't you think just one would have been sufficient?"

"I thought one might know something another didn't," she said, and sniffed again. Thinking of Edith, I told her to get some Kleenex and stop sniffing.

"The papers are horrible," she said, and I told her that papers like to sensationalize. I picked one up off the stack. The screamer headline read, FORT WORTH MILLIONAIRE SLAYS ENTIRE FAMILY. The subheadline added, SHOTGUN MURDERS SHOCK RIDGLEA.

"I call that libel, myself," I commented and tossed the paper back down on the coffee table.

"What does that mean?" Becky sniffed, and I told her I wouldn't tell her until she got some Kleenex.

She got some Kleenex.

Then I explained, "Nobody has proven yet that Olead killed anybody. And whoever did it didn't kill an entire family, because there's a fifteen-month-old baby unharmed."

"But can't you get him out of *jail?*" she wailed, and I told her if I could I would but obviously I could not. I went in the kitchen to make supper.

Hal came in with his Pac-Man watch and Becky

screamed at him to get that awful noise out of the living room. I invited Becky to go to her own room until she could calm down, and she screamed, "He doesn't have to play Pac-Man in the living room all the time!"

"And you don't have to scream in the living room all the time, either," I told her.

"I don't scream all the time," she screamed.

"I know you don't. And Hal doesn't play Pac-Man all the time, either. Now settle down, Becky, you're not doing Olead any good with this kind of nonsense."

"Then how can I do him any good?" she demanded.

"By letting me have some peace and quiet so I can get some rest so my brain will be able to function tomorrow," I told her tartly, and she sniffed again and reopened a newspaper.

Feeling like doing a little screaming myself, I got out a pound of hamburger and started cutting the onions to make a meat loaf. Normally I would have asked Becky to peel the potatoes, but I didn't feel like having her follow me around the kitchen sniffing, so I peeled the potatoes myself and got a can of green beans out of the pantry. And the telephone rang.

I thought it would be my son-in-law to tell me Vicky had finally decided to go to the hospital, but it was only Harry to say apologetically that he was sorry he had forgotten to tell me, but he had to go to the lodge and help out with bingo because a couple of their regular workers were out of town. He asked me if I didn't want to come out and play.

I told him I had already started making supper and no, I did not want to go play bingo.

He told me Becky could finish making supper for herself and Hal, and he thought maybe we could go to Joe T. Garcia's for supper. That, he added helpfully, should help me get my mind off things.

I told him Becky didn't seem to be in a very good mood, and besides that if we went to Joe T. Garcia's we'd never get to the lodge in time for bingo.

He said okay, if I felt that way. He sounded hurt.

Of course I told Becky to finish making the meat loaf for herself and Hal, and I went over to Joe T. Garcia's, and Harry and I stood in line outside for ten minutes and we stood in line inside for fifteen minutes. But the ordering process is greatly simplified at Joe T. Garcia's, mainly because you do not order at all; they bring everybody the same meal; and so we were only fifteen minutes late for bingo at the Elks Lodge. Harry grabbed a handful of paper cards and went wandering around selling them, and I got some cards to play and sat down. Then I got back up and got a beer.

I don't smoke, and I despise a smoke-filled room, which of course the bingo hall always is. When I left (without winning; I never win at bingo), I went straight home and washed my hair in the shower to get all the smoke out. When I got out of the shower and started to blow-dry my hair, Harry came in and told me Don had just called to say very excitedly that he was taking Vicky to Glenview Hospital.

So of course Harry and I rushed over to Glenview Hospital and stayed out there until around 3:00 A.M when the doctor decided it had been a false alarm and sent Vicky back home to wait a while longer.

Need I say that I was not fully awake the next morning when the telephone rang at six o'clock? I should have been awake by then, but I wasn't, and I tripped over the cat on my way to the phone. Captain Millner said they were calling out the whole major case squad, at the request of the FBI, because we had a kidnapped bank vice president.

I protested to Captain Millner that I didn't need to be on that because I was already on a major case of my own. "For which we already have a suspect in custody," Captain Millner reminded me. "Come on out, Deb. The FBI requests—"

What the FBI wants, the FBI generally manages to get. Harry made me a cup of instant coffee while I tried to get my eyes open. I crawled into a beige pants suit and then took the jacket back off to put on my shoulder holster. From what I read in books, some plainclothes policewomen still carry their pistols in their purses. Not me. For one thing, a purse could be taken away from me a little too easily. But the main reason I use a shoulder holster dates back to the night I had been driving with my overcoat on, and since I didn't want to juggle my purse and my overcoat, I had taken the pistol out of my purse and dropped it into the outside pocket of the coat.

Later on, it started to get warm in the car, and I took the coat off and laid it over on the seat. About half an hour after that, dispatch broadcast a lookout for an armed robbery suspect from a holdup of a liquor store on Berry Street, and just as he finished the broadcast I spotted a car fitting the description.

Using the flashing light on my dash, I pulled the car over. Grabbing my ID out of my purse, I headed for the suspect vehicle, and I was nearly to it when I remembered where my pistol was.

Fortunately for me, that wasn't the right car. But as I retrieved my pistol, I promised myself I would have a shoulder holster before I went on duty the next day. And I had one, and I've worn it ever since. It's comfortable. You can almost forget you have it on.

But the problem with that is, you also can almost forget you don't have it on, if you're staggering around half asleep as I was that morning.

Anyway, I had it on now, as I parked my car at the police station and went inside long enough to get the key to a detective car to drive on out to the bank. I thought I knew every bank in Fort Worth, but I couldn't ever remember hearing of this one. The First Federated Bank of Ridglea.

Well, if it was a bank it had money, and if it was a bank in Ridglea most likely it had a lot of money.

There were two uniform cars there, two FBI cars, three detective cars, a fire truck, and a white Cadillac, last year's model. They were all parked outside the small brick building. This bank was housed by itself, which was a little unusual; most banks now seem to build enormous office complexes and then rent out about ninety percent of the space to assorted small businesses.

As I drove around the bank to park, I saw there was also an ambulance. That explained the fire truck, I guessed. Fort Worth has the quaint custom of dispatching a pumper on almost every ambulance call, for reasons never adequately explained to me. (Actually I think it's because the firemen are trained paramedics. But I still don't see why they can't just leave the ambulance people to do their own work.)

At the door I stood and waited until a patrolman opened it from the inside. He locked it again behind me.

Inside, I sniffed. "What's the smoke?" I asked. Maybe the fire truck wasn't there just because of the ambulance this time.

"We've had a little fire," Captain Millner told me.

I don't know how he does it. He had to have left home as much too early as I did, but he managed as always to look shaved, combed, and put together. I was quite aware I did not look put together this morning.

But then, neither did the First Federated Bank of Ridglea.

A man in a disheveled gray striped suit sat droopily on the floor, with two emergency medical technicians hovering over him, one of them holding an ice pack to the side of his head. The detectives and the FBI agents were sort of wandering around doing nothing in particular, and an ident tech was wading in water and burned paper to fingerprint an open vault door. The stench of burning plastic seemed to come from several rolls of computer tape in the burned area.

This is silly, I thought, looking at the quite unoccupied people already there. They didn't need me on this. "What happened?" I asked.

"Have I got to tell it *again*?" the man sitting on the floor demanded fretfully.

"No, sir, you don't have to tell it again," Captain Millner told him. "At least not now."

"Who's she?" asked an FBI agent, in what he apparently thought was a subdued voice. I had never met him, but he had to be an FBI agent. Either that or a Mormon missionary. Have you ever noticed that? FBI agents and Mormon missionaries dress just alike, with short military haircuts and dark suits and white shirts and very subdued neckties. They look like they're cut out with cookie cutters that stop when they get to faces.

This man was young enough to be a Mormon missionary, but Mormon missionaries don't wear guns.

"She's a detective on the major case squad," Captain Millner told him.

"She doesn't look like a detective to me," the agent said.

I started to tell him he didn't look to me like an FBI agent, either, but I didn't. I was tired, but not tired enough to be that reckless.

"Here's what we've got, Deb," Millner said. "This gentleman is Slade Blackburn. He's the vice president—or rather, *a* vice president—of this bank. He tells us that this morning his wife was feeling ill, so instead of having breakfast at home he was going to go to a waffle house to avoid disturbing her. He left the house quite a lot earlier than usual. When he stepped outside, somebody stuck a gun in his back, took his car keys away from him, and forced him into the back of a laundry truck. They drove over here to the bank, with one of them driving his car, and ordered him to open the door. Then they ordered him to open the vault. He told them it was on a time lock that couldn't be opened until eight-thirty, and they told him he'd better figure out how to open it, because they'd left somebody with his wife in case he decided to get cute. So he opened the vault and they took a lot of money and threw papers and computer tapes around and set fire to some of them, and then hit him over the head with something and knocked him out. When he came to, he called the FBI and the FBI called us."

"And what I want to know," Slade Blackburn said from the floor, "is when is somebody going to go over there and see if my wife is all right?"

"Mr. Blackburn, I've asked you your address three times," one of the FBI men said, not too patiently.

He gave his address this time, and I said, "I'll go."

"I'll go with you," said the FBI man who didn't think I looked like a detective.

In the car, he said, "I didn't mean to be rude. But you really don't look like a detective."

"Oh, I know that," I assured him, and decided that since he was acting more friendly now I'd tell him what he looked like to me.

He laughed at that. "Well, I'm not a Mormon missionary," he said. "My name is Eddie Cohen, and my daddy is a rabbi."

"Okay," I said. "Anyhow, I said I never saw a Mormon missionary with a gun. In case nobody told you, I'm Deb Ralston."

We were in my car; Eddie had arrived at the bank with another FBI agent. I turned right onto Lackland and right again onto Elizabeth Lane and nearly got lost for a minute, because that was several blocks before I should have turned. But then I got sorted out again and found the address, over sort of behind the Ridglea Christian Church. It was a big, sprawling brick ranch-style house, maybe twenty years old. It had a nice lawn and nice trees and nice shrubbery and a nice white Cadillac (this year's model) parked on the nice gravel driveway. It looked too high-class a house for its neighborhood, and it looked completely undisturbed. The newspaper was lying on the lawn, folded up so tightly it seemed to be tied in a knot.

Eddie knocked on the door. "FBI," he shouted. "Mrs. Blackburn, are you there?"

I had asked Blackburn to tell me where the master bedroom was. I went and knocked on the windows of it. "Police," I called. "Mrs. Blackburn?"

Eddie tried the door. It was locked. "I'll check the back," I said.

The back door was locked, too. I tried to open the

garage, but it was controlled by an electronic door opener and it wouldn't open.

I went back to the front door.

"What now?" Eddie asked me.

I got on my radio and asked dispatch to call the house and ask Mrs. Blackburn to open the door. In a minute I could hear the telephone ringing, but nobody was moving around inside to answer it. Finally dispatch said, "We're getting no answer."

The phone stopped ringing.

"Do you know how to kick a door open?" I asked Eddie.

"Theoretically," he said. "But I've never seen it done."

"I've seen it done, but I'm not big enough to do it."

He caught hold of my arm to help him keep his balance. He planted his right foot against the door and pushed, hard, and the door popped open.

We walked in.

It was a pleasant house, clean and too cool, as if somebody had turned the central heat down for the night and not turned it up again in the morning.

We turned down the hall to the right, to the front corner bedroom Blackburn said his wife slept in. And we found out why Mrs. Blackburn hadn't come to the door, or answered her telephone.

She was still in bed, lying on her back in a pink nylon nightgown, with cold cream on her face and her hair done up in plastic curlers covered with a pink ruffled dotted swiss cap. Her teeth were in a tooth jar on the bedside table, and beside the jar she had a box of Kleenex, a thermometer, a water glass, and a bottle of Nyquil.

She hadn't moved for the doorbell or the telephone because she'd been shot, once, through the right temple.

6

Eddie Cohen was a rookie, but he was an FBI-trained rookie. He put his hand over his mouth and dashed for the front door; I could hear him outside, and then I heard water running from the outside faucet. He came back in, his head high, and he didn't apologize. I didn't say anything either.

I went and got a fingerprint kit out of the car and dusted the telephone in the far end of the house. While I was lifting what few legible prints there were, Eddie asked, "Doesn't it bother you?"

I didn't pretend not to know what he meant. "No, not much," I told him.

"Then why does it bother me?" he demanded.

"Because you've never seen anything like it before. It bothers most people, the first time."

"But I've seen films of the FBI disaster squad," he argued.

"So have I. But they were films. This isn't."

Now that I was sure this telephone was free of fingerprints, I used it to call the bank and tell Captain Millner what we had found. I didn't want Blackburn to hear it first from one of the many police radios there were in the bank, although I somehow didn't expect Blackburn was going to be terribly surprised by the news.

Then I called dispatch, also on the telephone, and told them to get me somebody from the medical examiner's office and a crime scene crew.

The bank robbery belonged to the feds. The murder in the house belonged to us; more specifically, because I was the first detective on the scene, it belonged to me.

When Millner arrived, about the same time as the medical examiner's investigator, I tried to argue with him about that. I reminded him that I was in the major case squad; by rights, this ought to be worked by homicide.

Millner regarded me disgustedly, and I reminded myself that he hadn't wanted a woman on the major case squad, or on homicide. He had been afraid a woman couldn't cope with this kind of work, and he hadn't admitted yet that I had proven him wrong on that. "Deb," he said now, "shut up."

I decided I had better not argue any more.

The man from the medical examiner's office declared Joan Blackburn dead. I did not say "No shit, Sherlock," but I thought it.

The crime scene people took pictures and the medical examiner's investigator said he was ready to have the body moved. "In a minute," I said. "Captain, I want you to have a look at this body."

He had a look at that body. Then he looked at me, moodily. "So?" he said.

"See what I mean?" I asked.

"Yeah," he answered. "Well, it was no more than I expected."

"What are you talking about?" Eddie demanded.

"Nothing I'd expect you to be able to spot, no more experience than you've got," Millner told him, and turned to the medical examiner's investigator and the transport crew. "Sanchez," he said, "suppose I told you that woman had been seen alive at six o'clock this morning, what would you say?"

Sanchez looked at the body. "You gotta be kidding," he said.

"Then let me put it another way," Millner said. "Suppose I told you the victim's husband says he saw that woman alive at six o'clock this morning, what would you say?"

Sanchez looked at the body again. "I'd say he's a liar," he said. "Just for starters."

"Be sure you keep that in mind," Millner told him. "Because I'll be asking you for an official estimate. What about you, Olsen?"

Olsen, who is on the transport crew only until there is an opening for another investigator, removed a rectal thermometer he had inserted in the body on arrival and looked at it, looked at a room thermometer he had set on a dressing table. "Four A.M. at the latest," he said. "But that's pushing it and remembering it's cool in here. She was under two blankets, though. No later than four A.M. But more like three, three-thirty."

"I want it in writing," Millner said.

"You'll get it in writing," Sanchez said.

"Can we take the body now?" Olsen asked. "Because we got another call."

We agreed they could take the body.

When they moved the body, they found an exit wound a lot larger than the entry wound. That is nothing unusual. They waited for Irene to photograph the wound, and then they put the body in a black plastic body bag and they put the body bag on the gurney, and then they asked one of the crime scene people to try to find the slug. The ME would like to know what caliber it was.

Irene Loukas, who had been waiting impatiently for them to move the body so she could get back to work on the crime scene, dug down in the mattress with a scalpel and located the slug. It was squat and big around. "Forty-five," she said, turning it over curiously in a gloved hand.

"Have you got anything to say it looks like automatic or revolver?" I asked, which was a rather silly question and I knew it as soon as I asked.

Irene looked at me pityingly and said, "Really, Deb."

"Automatic," her partner Bob Castle said triumphantly.

He grabbed the camera, which was lying on the bed where Irene had left it after photographing the exit wound. He took photographs, and he and Irene took measurements and made notes, and then Bob picked up the expended shell from near the closet door and turned it over. The little scar from the ejection mechanism was quite evident. "Do you want to take it and the slug in?" he asked the ME's investigator.

"Uh-uh," Sanchez told him. "Wait till you've got a pistol to send with it, and then send it to the firearms examiner."

"We'd never have guessed, dumbass," Irene said.

"Well, I didn't know," Bob protested. "Last time I had a murder you wanted the ejected shell."

"Because the slug was still inside the head," Sanchez reminded him, and they left with the body.

Irene and Bob resumed work on the crime scene, and I went out to start canvassing the neighborhood, with Eddie tagging along because he didn't have any way to get back to the bank or his office until I was ready to go. It would have helped if the Blackburn house had been on a dead-end street, or a cul-de-sac, but it wasn't; it was on a street that ran for about a mile between Camp Bowie, which is one of the busiest four-lanes in Fort Worth, and the West Freeway, which is Fort Worth's share of a major east-west artery. That meant that whoever did this didn't have to be visible long and didn't have any shortage of escape routes. And there are not usually very many people out in their front yards at four—or even six—in the morning to see anything that might be visible.

Of the people we managed to catch at home (roughly one house out of six; despite the Ridglea area, this was a working-class neighborhood), nobody had seen anything. Especially not a laundry truck, name of laundry unknown. Nobody had heard a shot. Nobody knew what we were talking about.

But they were *very* impressed with Eddie's identification. Mine didn't interest anybody much. Fort Worth police they see every day.

I went back to the bank to leave Eddie with the FBI

and to see whether I could talk with Slade Blackburn, but he, I was informed, was at John Peter Smith Hospital, being treated for concussion and shock.

Shock, my eye, I thought, and wondered why nobody had heard the shot. A forty-five is loud, not quite as loud as a shotgun but plenty loud enough, and at six or six-thirty, which was when the shot supposedly was fired, people are already awake and stirring.

Somebody should have heard it, if that had been when it was fired. Which of course it wasn't.

Somebody had heard a shot from Olead's house. Of course that was a shotgun, but it was at three o'clock in the morning and everybody was asleep and, on New Year's Eve, probably most of them had good reason to be sleeping soundly.

Somebody reported hearing *a* shot from Olead's house. Not five shots. Not a burst of shooting. A shot.

And there was no way in the world all that furniture was heaped up in that one room between the time that shot was heard and the time Shea arrived to start banging on the door.

Besides that, when I got there before 4:00 A.M. I would have been willing to swear the victims had been dead over two hours. Yes, damn it, I know they had, because they were cooling considerably. Postmortem lividity had begun, and that happens before rigor mortis, but all the same it doesn't happen instantly.

The shot that neighbor heard was not a shot that killed anybody. It was an extra shot. There were six shots fired in that house that night. Not five, six.

I couldn't do any more on the Blackburn killing right now, not until I could talk with Blackburn, the FBI, and the rest of my squad, and see what everybody had and how it seemed to fit together. I wanted to search Blackburn's house, but strictly speaking only the bedroom was the crime scene, and I didn't want to tip our hand yet by asking for a search warrant.

Although we'd have to do it before Blackburn got a chance to go home.

Probably nothing was hidden at his house; probably he

had it all somewhere else. For all I knew, he might have everything stashed in a nice safety deposit box at his own bank. But on the other hand he could be stupid enough, and confident enough, that he'd left the gun on a closet shelf.

But while I was waiting to get on with that, I went back into my office and called up all the files on Olead's case.

We don't keep case files per se anymore. I miss that. Everything's on a computer, and when you want to read the reports you ask for printouts. But if you're like me you sometimes want to reread the reports, and reread them, and so when I'm deeply involved with a case I usually keep my own case file, in my desk drawer. But I hadn't made one yet about Olead, because I had been doing so many other things.

The original call came from a neighbor. All the calls coming into dispatch are taped, and on an uneventful night, the tapes will be routinely saved a certain length of time and then erased and reused. But any time something big goes down, the tape is held. Eventually, the important excerpt is spliced out for the rest of the tape to be reused. But the result is that in a situation like this I can go and listen to the call myself; I don't have to depend on somebody's written report, or possibly faulty memory, for details of the call.

I went and asked to hear the tape.

The sound of a phone ringing. "Fort Worth Police emergency line." A young man's voice; the assignment log for the night would tell me whose, if the tape cut wasn't labeled. I checked; it was. Reuben Dakle.

"This is Arlon Powers. I don't know if I'm calling the right number or not."

"Well, suppose you tell me the problem." Reuben Dakle was patient. People calling the police often aren't sure whether they should be, especially on New Year's Eve.

"I'm not sure, but I think I just heard a shot from the house next door."

"Yes, sir, what address was that? What is your telephone number, in case we need to call you back? What is your name? Do you want the officer to contact you?"

Powers didn't sound drunk, particularly; he might have come home drunk, but he'd have been sleeping it off. He didn't have his window open. His house was on the west side of the Carsons' house. His bedroom was on the east side of his house. He heard only one shot. Yes, he was sure it was a shot. It was a shotgun. He'd been thinking about it, and yes, he was sure.

Routinely, Danny Shea had been dispatched to check it out.

Shea went to the Powers home first, before he went to the Carson home, because he wasn't too keen on waking somebody up at three o'clock in the morning for what might prove to be a mare's-nest. But, interviewed, Arlon Powers had been more positive than he had sounded on the tape. He had heard a shot. It was a shotgun, probably a twelve-gauge. He knew it came from Jack Carson's house. He had been kind of nervous about that house anyway, because he'd heard that Mrs. Carson's son was some kind of a psycho. Well, he seemed nice enough to talk with, but you never knew.

I thought I would like to talk with Arlon Powers.

Shea was supposed to have gotten a work address and telephone number for the complainant, but that didn't mean he had. If not, I'd have to find out. The Carson house, big and expensive as it was, was sandwiched between two bungalows, and of course the call had come from one or the other.

But maybe I'd be lucky. Maybe Danny Shea had gotten all the information he was supposed to get.

I checked.

I was lucky.

Arlon Powers was an installation foreman at Southwestern Bell. His work address was 1116 Houston, and he'd be there if he wasn't out on a job site.

Well, I thought, that would be convenient if he wasn't out on a job site, because that location is just about a block from the police station. I called his work number. Arlon Powers was in his office, and sure, he had plenty of time to talk with me.

His office was littered with work orders and coils of wire and pieces of telephone sets, some boxed, some not, and for the first five minutes I was there he wanted to gripe about how the restructure of the telephone company had messed things up. I agreed with him that court orders sometimes aren't very realistic, and asked if we could talk about New Year's Eve.

He told me I didn't look like a detective.

I agreed that I didn't look like a detective, and said, "Now, about New Year's Eve—"

He asked if I wanted some coffee, and I told him not really, because I really needed to talk with him.

He said if I didn't mind he'd get some himself. He set about making instant coffee, with speed more deliberate than fast, and I reminded myself my dentist had told me to stop grinding my teeth.

"Now," he said finally, "about New Year's Eve. I had been kind of worrying even before that happened, because I'd heard the boy was some kind of a psycho, but you never know about rumors, and he's always seemed easy enough to talk with. And the way he takes care of them two kids is something *else*, I want to tell you."

I said oh, really, and Powers said, "Oh, yes, taking them for walks, playing with them in the yard—you just don't often see a young man that concerned about kids. But—you wanted to know about that shot I heard, right?"

"Yes, sir. You told the dispatcher you heard one shot. Is that right?"

"That's what I heard," he said firmly. "I know the newspapers say they was five people killed—that's terrible, you know it?—but I didn't hear but the one shot. And it sounded kindly loud to be coming from inside the house. You ask me, I'd have said it was coming from the back yard, except that I looked back there the second I heard it and there was nobody in sight, except there was a screen off that one window, and so I decided it must have come from there."

"A screen off which window?" I asked. This was the first I had heard of that.

He thought about it. "Well, my house is set back some from the Carsons', you know, and so from my side window I can see the back of their house. It'd be—um—the—" He frowned, cocked his head over; he was thinking. The frown cleared up. "It'd be the third window from my end on the back."

The third window from the west end. Olead's bedroom window. "Why didn't you tell the officer that, when he went to see you?"

"Well, I did, but he said it wasn't important."

I think I may kill Danny Shea. I really think I may kill him, I thought. "Is there anything else you told him that he said wasn't important?" I asked.

"Well, yes'm, there was," he said. "And it kindly puzzled me, because I thought as how it was important. About a minute, minute and a half, after I heard the shot I heard a door slam at the back of the house."

"Could you see what door?"

"No'm, because by that time I was on the phone reporting the shot. But best as I can tell, I think it was that back door going out of the den onto the patio."

And Shea didn't think that was important.

At least the rest of us had waited until we walked into the house before deciding Olead had done it. But Shea hadn't even done that. He'd heard Powers say "some kind of psycho" and he'd made up his mind then; and he hadn't mentioned to anybody anything that could have altered that theory.

"Mr. Powers, I appreciate very much what you've told me," I said. "Could you spare the time to come over to the police station and let me get a written statement of it?"

"Is it important, then?"

"Yes, sir, it is important," I said grimly.

"Well, I thought as how it ought to be important, but that young officer, he said—"

Shamelessly using my age as an advantage, I answered, "Well, Mr. Powers, you and I know these young people always think they know more than they do."

All the way to the police station Mr. Powers told me

stories about the iniquities of the system and the way young people can get away with things they shouldn't ought to get away with, and he told me the same stories all the way back to the telephone company building. But it was worth it. I had a statement, and for the first time I had something concrete to back up my theory that there must have been somebody else in the house that night.

I put all the necessary vitamins for Olead for one day in an envelope and folded it shut and put it in my jacket pocket. Then I drove over to the county jail and told them I needed to see Olead Baker.

The shift officer at the jail looked at me sourly. "You'll talk to him in his cell, then," he said. "We've had to isolate him from the rest of the jail population."

"Oh?" I said.

"Yeah," the shift officer said and directed somebody to take me to Olead's cell. I stopped by a vending machine and, remembering he'd said he couldn't handle much sugar, I got a diet Dr. Pepper in a paper cup and took it along.

I'd never seen a padded cell before, but this was definitely a padded cell. It was small, there wasn't a speck of furniture in it, and all sides, even the roof and floor, were covered with tan vinyl mattresses. Despite the incredible fetid stench, Olead, in jail coveralls, was lying comfortably on the floor with his bare feet dug into the mattress on one wall and one arm under his head, unconcernedly reading. He put down the book and sat up when I came in.

"Bang on the bars when you want out," the jailer told me, and locked the door.

"What on earth happened to you?" I exclaimed.

Olead had a black eye, a cut lip, and assorted other bruises and contusions, mostly on his face. He grinned at me. "That should be fairly obvious," he answered. "Clearly, I'm growing a beard."

I sat down, cross-legged, on the floor. I didn't like sitting there, but I didn't intend to try to keep my balance on the mattresses. It made me feel drunk to try.

I gave him the drink and the envelope of vitamins, and he swallowed the vitamins and then drained the cup. "Thank you," he said. "Deb, I hope you know how much I appreciate this."

"That's okay," I said. "Olead, who did that?"

"It doesn't matter," he said.

"It does too matter!"

He shook his head. "The guards broke it up, and they put me in here where nobody else could get at me. I've been in a padded cell before, probably in this one before; that doesn't bother me much. It won't happen again."

"Olead, I want to know who did it."

"I'm not going to tell you," he answered. "Look, even criminals don't like people who harm children. They did this thinking they were doing it to the person who killed Brenda, and since this is just a little tiny sample of what I'd like to do to the person who killed Brenda, I'm not going to tell on them. I don't appreciate being mistaken for a child murderer, but they're not the only ones making that mistake, and I do appreciate knowing that even people who didn't know her care that much about what happened to her. So forget it, Deb, I'm not going to tell you."

That was about as final as he could get.

"All right, be that way," I said, and he grinned again. "I want to ask you something else," I added. "Have you had the window screen off your bedroom window?"

"No," he said, "why would I do that?"

"I have a witness who says the screen was off your bedroom window the night of the shootings," I told him.

He frowned. "I don't know any reason why it would have been. If you're going to try to say somebody came in that way, forget it. You know my bed is right by that window, and they'd have had to climb right over me. I'd know if somebody did that."

"And you didn't have the screen off for any reason? Did you hear a door slam maybe fifteen, twenty minutes before Shea woke you up?"

"Deb," he said, "if I didn't hear five shotgun blasts I didn't hear a door slam."

That was reasonable enough.

"Olead," I said, "keep trying to remember. Even if you dream something and you know it's distorted because it's a dream, tell me about it; it might give me something to go on."

"I'll do it," he said, "but I don't dream. I mean, I guess I dream because everybody does, but I've got some kind of block against remembering dreams."

"Okay. See you later." I banged on the bars, and somebody came and let me out.

"Hey," Olead said to the jailer, "can I have the telephone again?"

"Buddy, you've had the telephone an hour today," the jailer told him.

"I know," Olead said, "but now I want it again."

The jailer shrugged. He picked up one of several telephone sets with very long cords. He unplugged the cord from the set, threaded the cord through the bars of the one small window in the front of the padded steel door, and plugged the cord back into the set. He closed the door, and Olead headed off into the corner of the cell with the telephone. "Now you remember, Baker," the jailer shouted through the bars, "if somebody else asks for that, I got to have it back."

"Yeah, I know," Olead said. As I stood in the hall and waited for the jailer to finish threading the long cord into the cell so that nobody would trip over it, I heard Olead dialing, and then I heard his soft voice saying, "Becky?"

Oh, great, I thought. She'll be impossible again this evening.

Then I wondered what it was that seemed different about Olead, and then I realized. He didn't act fifteen anymore; he'd emotionally caught up with himself. He was twenty-six, and he acted twenty-six. I wondered why. It wasn't because of jail; he'd been confined before. And it wasn't because of the beating, because he'd been hurt before.

Was it the grief?

Or was it Becky?

I went back to my office, and Irene called me from ident and said, "Dave drove the evidence to Austin and nagged them into doing the tests today. I wanted to see if you were back in, so I could send the reports up to you."

"I'm back in," I said. "And I'll come down there."

You would think that the detective bureau and ident, since they work so closely together, would be on the same floor. But the detective bureau is on the third floor, and ident is in the basement. I went down there, this time riding the elevator without the bullet hole, and Irene handed me Xerox copies of the lab reports.

I hunted the one about the carpet fragment. Human vomitus, sample inadequate to tell what type of food had been involved, particularly in view of the fact that digestion was well advanced. But what was certain was that there was a quantity of Mellaril present, quantity sufficient to indicate subject had ingested a severe overdose. Urine also contained traces of Mellaril, I found, turning to that report.

Mellaril, I thought, and asked Irene if she had a *Physician's Desk Reference*. She had an old one, inherited from the narcs when they got their new one, and I looked up Mellaril. And I found that it was a sedative often used to treat mental and emotional disturbances. Something he might reasonably have taken, although probably not recently.

Then I turned to the next lab report, the one on the gunpowder residue test.

It was exactly what I had expected.

The bruise on his shoulder already had told me.

But for some reason I still found it a shock to read it on the report.

There was no doubt whatever that Olead Baker, no matter what he said, no matter what he remembered, had fired a shotgun on New Year's Eve.

7

I remember thinking, what if I'm wrong?

I'm no psychiatrist. I don't know anything about how these things work, schizophrenia, psychosis. Could he have flipped out, killed them, and forgotten it? Is that possible?

Either he did, or he didn't. Whether he did or he didn't, he wasn't guilty—not morally, because if he did do it he didn't know what he was doing, if he did do it he was now totally unconscious of having done it.

I had already concluded there had to be a sixth shot, and he had to have fired that sixth shot. If he did kill them, of course he fired all six shots, and if he didn't kill them, there was absolutely, positively, certainly no other way for that bruise to get on his shoulder, that gunpowder residue to get on his hands. But who did he fire that shot at, and why didn't he remember?

And really, could I assume that the fact that he had to have fired the sixth shot proved that he didn't fire the other five?

I'd have to think about it later, but now I was too tired.

I looked at my watch. It was no wonder I was too tired. It was five o'clock, and I was supposed to get off at four. The rest of my squad wasn't still out on the Blackburn case, as I'd supposed. They'd undoubtedly already left.

I went home and made salmon croquettes and green peas for supper (and of course the peas made me think of Brenda crying about eating peas for supper on her last night of life). I tried to pretend everything was normal, which was very hard to do with Becky looking at me reproachfully every five seconds. She didn't even seem interested in reading the new catalogs she had sent for. I asked her if she'd had a chance to try out her credit card yet, and she said, "No." No explanation. No discussion of when she would get to the store. Just no.

Hal, on the other hand, wouldn't stop talking. Apparently he and his friends had discussed nothing else but the killlings all day at school, and they had not only uncritically swallowed everything the newspapers had said, but then had proceeded to embroider the stories.

And definitely Olead was continuing to make news. He'd even crowded Cullen Davis off the front page. I supposed Cullen Davis might be grateful for that; the best I could remember, he'd made the front page at least once a week for the last four years. It crossed my mind to wonder if he was sympathizing with Olead. Personally, I had always wondered if he might have been set up too, though I never could decide who by, or why.

Of course, he never was my case, which was probably just as well.

But I didn't figure anybody could guess from the papers that there was anybody at all, in or out of the police department, who guessed Olead Baker might have been set up.

If there was just some way of figuring out *why*—

Hal said something under his breath and snickered, and Harry said sharply, "That's enough, son," just as Becky burst into tears and ran away from the table.

"Oh, *damn*," Harry said explosively. "Hal, why don't you use a little bit of common sense? The fact that the paper says something doesn't make it true, and your sister has spent the last two hours talking with that man on the telephone. That in itself should indicate to you that it's not to be treated as a joke. If you don't have any common sense or tact, at least try to have a little compassion for Becky."

Hal asked what compassion was, and Harry started explaining. I began to clear the table without trying to serve any dessert. But after a while Hal went and told Becky he was sorry, and Becky sniffed and said that was okay, and Hal went and got some ice cream out of the freezer.

I think that kid could eat ice cream in an earthquake.

Harry turned on the television, and I watched until ten-thirty without the faintest idea what was going on. We went to bed as soon as the news was over, and Harry at once started snoring. I could have wrung his neck. I pulled a pillow over my head, which didn't help. I decided to go and sleep on the couch, but then I couldn't get at the extra blankets, because they were still in Harry's truck from the last time he and Hal went camping. So I got a beach towel out of the linen closet to use for a cover, and lay down on the couch, and the cat started walking up and down on my back. I gave up and went back to bed.

Harry went on snoring, and then I started feeling guilty that I was being so cross about Harry snoring and the cat walking on my back, when Olead was sleeping on the floor in that stinking jail cell without a sheet or blanket or anything. But maybe they would give him one at night.

I hoped so.

I wasn't really in very good shape when I got to work the next day, but everybody charitably pretended not to notice. Or maybe they really didn't notice. There were two FBI agents, a fire inspector, and the head of homicide (who clearly was not over his flu) all crowded into our four-desk office, along with the six members of the major case squad who of course belonged there.

The fire inspector cleared his throat importantly. He likes to clear his throat importantly; it impresses juries, but it tends to drive his fellow officers totally bananas. Then he said, "We have determined that the fire in the bank began at approximately five A.M."

"Oh, really?" one of the FBI agents said, in a pleased voice. "Would you explain that, please?"

He at once became highly technical about two-hour fire ratings and a board that had burned three-quarters of the way through before the fire department arrived, which proved something or other, I was a little hazy as to what. But the upshot of the explanation seemed to be that he could definitely demonstrate to a jury that the fire in the vault had begun half an hour before Blackburn said that he had come out of the front door and been kidnapped.

Which made Slade Blackburn a liar.

Again.

That, we agreed, provided us with adequate probable cause to get a search warrant. We wrangled for a while over whether to get a state search warrant or a federal one, but we came to the conclusion that we were far more likely to be able to prove the murder than the bank robbery. Captain Millner agreed to take out the search warrant himself.

Somebody called the hospital and found Blackburn was due to be released at eleven, so we decided we'd be at his house waiting for him. One FBI agent would be at the bank, in case he went there first, and one would follow his car. Just generally in case.

Eleven, and it was nine now. I decided to go off in a corner and try to put everything together about Olead, which I had started several times before to do and always gotten interrupted.

Unfortunately, there is no such thing as a quiet corner in the police department. The building is unbelievably over-crowded. They have promised us a new one—well, it's more than a promise, I think the construction has already begun—but all the same, it's at least a year before we'll be in it. On a pretty sunny day I could go sit at the Water Garden and think, but it was about thirty-eight degrees and threatening sleet, snow, or other nasties. Finally I took my notebook and clipboard and went over to the jail and asked to be taken to Olead's cell.

He was reading, as usual lying on his back with his feet halfway up the opposite wall and the book on his chest. He put the book down when I came in. "Hi," he said, sounding a little surprised. I had been getting over there in the afternoon.

I gave him his vitamins and his diet Dr. Pepper, and said, "Go on reading. I need to think and there's not a quiet place in the police station to do it."

He looked genuinely startled, and then he laughed softly. "Okay," he said, "it's reasonably quiet in here, I suppose. What do you need to think about?"

"We got the lab results back last night," I told him.

"Oh, really?" he said. "I thought that was going to take three weeks." He sat up, leaned back against the wall.

"Usually it would," I said. "They rushed it through. It's our DA's office, I think, Olead. Ever since last time they didn't convict Cullen Davis I've had a feeling the DA's office thinks the press thinks rich people get away with murder in Fort Worth. They want to convict a millionaire for something. Preferably murder, in order to prove the press is wrong. And now it looks like you're it."

"Damn the money," Olead said. "It hasn't done me much good. Who's Cullen Davis?"

I stared at him, astonished, and then realized he had been in no shape to pay attention to all of Cullen Davis's assorted trials and tribulations. I shrugged. "He's just a guy," I said. "One with a lot of money. He keeps getting acquitted of things."

"I'd better call him and ask how he does it," Olead said.

"He hires Racehorse Haynes, for one thing," I said. "That seems to help. You've got enough money. You can hire Racehorse Haynes if you want to."

"Who's Racehorse Haynes?" he asked.

"He's a high-caliber defense lawyer," I said. "I think he lives in Houston, but he comes to Fort Worth fairly often."

"Oh," Olead said vaguely. "Oh, I'm thinking about a lawyer."

"You should have had one at the committal hearing."

"They told me I should," he agreed, "but I didn't exactly want one right then. I'm thinking about it, though."

"Racehorse Haynes is real good," I told him. I had never had to come up against Racehorse Haynes in court. But if I ever had to, I'd rather do it in a case where I agreed with the defense. Then maybe I wouldn't get ulcers.

I'm told that Racehorse Haynes gives cops ulcers.

"Tell me the results of the lab tests, anyway," Olead urged. "Or are you not supposed to do that?"

"I'm not," I said. "However—"

He grinned.

"You had an overdose of Mellaril, for one thing," I told him. "That showed up in both the carpet sample from the bathroom, and in the urine test."

"What's Mellaril?" he asked. "Oh, wait a minute, I think I know—it's that stuff I used to have to take before I started taking Thorazine. How could I have gotten an overdose of Mellaril? I don't even have any."

"I don't know," I said, "but I think it's a question your attorney certainly should raise in court."

"I'll be sure and tell him, when I get one. How about breakfast? Could they tell I hadn't eaten breakfast?" I told him they couldn't, and he swore softly and said, "What about the gunpowder residue? It was negative, wasn't it?"

"No, Olead," I said, "it wasn't negative. And that's what I need to think about."

His face went pale. "You're kidding," he said. "Deb, you're kidding, aren't you?"

"I wish I was," I said. "The test was positive. Olead, I knew it was going to be, from that bruise on your shoulder. You have to have fired a shotgun that night."

He shook his head. "No," he said, "no, I did not."

"Olead," I said, my voice raised a little higher than I meant it to be, "will you please stop arguing and help me think? If you didn't fire a shotgun then how in the bloody *hell* did you get that bruise on your shoulder and that gunpowder residue on your hands? If you didn't kill them, then who did? We've got to figure out what happened that night, instead of arguing about facts."

He looked as if he had been slapped. Very quietly and steadily, he answered, "You think, Deb. You think and I'll read." He picked up his book again. The title of it was *Clinical Psychology.*

Some light reading for a man in a padded cell.

I should have realized why he was upset, but I didn't, not then. I started doodling stars and oyster shells on my paper and thinking, sitting on the floor of Olead's isolation cell with my shoes off, leaning back on a side wall. Olead, leaning against the opposite wall, concentrated on his book, glancing at me every now and then with a hurt look on his face.

All right, I told myself, try to put this together. There were four shots fired in the den, and four empties were picked up in there. They were all Federals, possibly from the half-empty box in the house, and they all matched the remaining shells in the 12-gauge Remington that was leaning against the wall between the kitchen and the den. The firearms examiner agreed they'd been fired from that shotgun. Now, those had to be the first shots, because it was utterly inconceivable that the four adults would have been sitting in the den after a shot was fired in a bedroom, not unless there were two killers; not unless the victims were being held at bay. And no, that wasn't right, because what happened in the den started suddenly; it started and ended so fast that Jake had time to pick up his gun but didn't have time to use it.

All right, the killer fired four shots, fast, in the den, and then he put the gun down and then he went with a different gun—definitely a different gun, because the firearms examiner said that old Winchester shell had been fired from the old Browning shotgun—into the bedroom and shot the child.

One child, not both children.

94

But one killer? Or two killers?

And all the time Olead was asleep. The killer—or killers—knew that; he had to have known it. He murdered a four-year old girl while her twenty-six-year-old half-brother, who loved the child dearly, slept in the room across the hall. And Olead is big and he's strong and he's fast; look at how he bucked off Shea when Shea tried to stop him from going after Jeffrey. I wouldn't want to tangle with Olead. Ergo, he knew Olead was asleep; he knew Olead wasn't going to wake up. And that means he is the one who doped Olead. He is the one who brought the Mellaril from somewhere outside the house and gave it to him—somehow.

Then he dragged all that stuff all over the bedroom to hide the baby, so we would think the baby was dead too. But that wasn't the whole reason. It couldn't be. That wouldn't make sense. Think some more.

Okay. This is a man who knew that Olead had been insane. And he knew that Olead had been afraid of cats. (I didn't even want to think about how the cat had been killed.) And he knew that Olead had once taken Mellaril. And he had some sort of access to Mellaril himself. And he knew about the time that Olead had wrecked the house. All right, that meant he had known the family a long time, because it had been seven years ago Olead wrecked the house, nine years ago he had stripped downtown because he saw a cat. Maybe a friend of Olead's mother, then?

No, that wouldn't work, because he didn't know that Olead was through being afraid of cats, and he didn't know that Olead was no longer taking Mellaril. So, not as close to the family as he had been. But still some close, close enough to know that Olead spent a lot of time with Jeffrey, loved Jeffrey, wouldn't hurt Jeffrey—but he didn't know Olead loved Brenda, why not? But still close enough to be invited over to the house for a party.

Maybe this would work. He was a friend of Olead's father. But Jack and Olead's father were—had been—friends, so he was a friend of both, or at least they knew him as a friend. But he knew Olead's father better than he knew Jack, so now he heard less of what was going on than he did when Olead's father was alive.

That didn't have to be true. He could be a closer friend of Jack. Because Jack wouldn't have as much to say about Olead as Olead's father did. That would stand to reason.

So—this was beginning to make some small amount of sense. He came to the party. And for some reason he decided—what could the reason be? That was the part that kept right on making no sense at all. For some reason he decided on this scheme to wipe out Olead's family, except for Jeffrey, and blame it on Olead. So he doped Olead—with Mellaril he had brought with him? That couldn't be right; people don't casually carry Mellaril around with them, not unless they're taking it themselves, and I hadn't come across anybody in this case likely to be taking Mellaril.

No, he had planned in advance, and that meant he knew in advance about the planned hunting trip. Had that happened before? Was it some kind of custom? I'd have to find that out. Anyhow, he came to the party. And he doped Olead. (How?) And he invited himself to go on the hunting trip. And then—

All right, but now I was back to the gunpowder on Olead's hands, the bruise on his shoulder. What had happened?

Say the killer was finishing up in the children's room; he dropped something; he woke Olead—Olead got hold of the gun and the killer ran out the door and Olead shot at him? That wouldn't work, though, because if he ran for the patio door Olead would have run after him—no. Maybe he wouldn't. Because his mother's body was lying just inside that door; the killer would have stepped over it but maybe Olead wouldn't—so he ran back to his room and fired through the bedroom window and the killer got away. And maybe that slam the telephone man heard wasn't the patio door; maybe it was the killer's car door, as he fled; and then Olead put the gun down and maybe fainted from the shock, and then went from the faint on into sleep, because he still had so much of the drug in his system—

Very nice. I had proved that Olead hadn't done it, except for one thing. Everything I had come up with could be turned the other way. Olead could have done every bit of it himself, including taking the Mellaril—from an old prescription—and he could have thrown the bottle away, or even taken it outside and buried it in the flower bed, and then when the stage was completely set and he was getting drowsy he could have fired out the bedroom window to be heard, counting on it the cops would come and find him asleep, drugged, the victim of a frame job.

He still could have done it himself.

The only thing was, he couldn't have been insane and done it.

Because whoever did it, the way it was done, it was a planned and premeditated crime, a sane crime. And I knew Olead couldn't have done it, because I knew Olead, but juries aren't supposed to take personalities into account.

Oh, damn, hell and damnation, the only way to prove Olead didn't do it was going to be to prove who did.

All right, a starting point, he was at the party, he had to be at the party, and he had to have access to something Olead was drinking—

The punch?

The punch that "tasted gross"?

"Olead," I asked, "who handed you the cup of punch?"

He looked up from his book. "What cup of punch?"

"At the party. That you didn't like."

"Oh. I don't remember. Mother, maybe, or somebody."

"Somebody like who?"

"Hell, who cares?" he said impatiently, and went back to reading.

"*I* care! If I didn't care I wouldn't be asking you," I pointed out crossly.

"Well, I'm sorry, but I don't know who," he answered.

97

"Olead, can you remember the name of one person, one single solitary person, who was at that party?"

He looked up again. "No, I can't," he answered shortly.

"Olead, you've got to help me," I almost pleaded. "Because if you didn't do it somebody else did, and it has to be somebody who was at that party."

He replied, this time without looking up, "If frogs had wings they wouldn't bump their tails when they hopped. I don't know who was at the party."

"You're not much help," I said, feeling thoroughly frustrated. "I guess I'll have to get your mother's address book and call everybody in it. Do you know where it is?"

"She didn't have one," he answered. "She's lived in Fort Worth all her life, and so have most of her friends. So usually when she had a party she just called people. If she decided to send out invitations she got the addresses out of the telephone book."

"Well, I certainly can't call everybody in the Fort Worth telephone book," I protested, standing up.

"Nobody asked you to," he retorted. "Look, Deb, I don't *know* who was at the party. If I did I'd tell you. I don't. I'm sorry. There's nothing I can do about it."

"Oh, I know," I said. "I'm sorry I'm so crabby. I'm just so darn frustrated."

He looked up, a wry expression on his face. "You know," he told me, "I can identify with that feeling." Whatever bad mood had caused his sulks apparently had dissipated, and he grinned at me.

"I'll see you later," I said.

He said, "Sure," a little absently and returned to his book.

"Where the hell have you been?" Captain Millner demanded. "You smell like a sewer!"

"Up talking to Olead Baker," I said. "They're keeping him isolated from the other prisoners because some of them were beating him up, and so they stuck him in that front padded cell. And there's nowhere else to sit but the floor, and you know what that cell smells like."

"I'd stand," Gary Hollister said fervently. "Look, my head is so stuffed up with this flu I can't smell anything, but even I can smell that. Take your own car to Blackburn's house; I'm darned if I'll ride with you."

"I had planned to take my own car," I answered with as much dignity as I could muster, quite aware I did indeed smell like a sewer.

Blackburn, when he got home, wasn't at all pleased to see us. He told us he was going to call his attorney. Captain Millner told him by all means to call his attorney, and we'd start searching while his attorney was on the way over. He told us we couldn't do that, and Millner said, "Watch us," and we fanned out and started searching.

I don't know what he was so antsy about. We searched his house and both cars, and we did not find any money. We did not find a .45. We did not find anything at all to link him to either crime.

What we did find that caused me to indulge in a lot of wishful thinking was a half box of old red paper Winchester shotgun shells, with no shotgun to use them in. But finally logic reasserted itself, as I remembered the half box of twenty-two-long rifle bullets in my dresser drawer to fit in a target pistol I sold ten years ago, and I reminded myself there was nothing at all to link the two cases together.

It would be interesting if there was, but there wasn't. And Blackburn practically sneered at us as we left.

I had to drop by the jail for something or other, I don't remember what now, something that related to another case I'd wound up just before Christmas, and I saw people waiting in line to visit prisoners.

Becky, in a blue car coat, was waiting in line.

We pretended not to see each other.

8

Halfway home that night, I remembered the other thing I should have looked into. There had been only five empty shotgun shells found, four Federals and a Winchester, and for my nice theory to work, there had to have been six. For any of my theories, actually; I had deduced a sixth shot half a dozen ways, half a dozen times.

The sixth empty, which ought to be a paper Winchester—but that wasn't sure, because I had jacked three plastic Federal shells out of that shotgun—would have to be somewhere in Olead's room. I was fairly sure nobody had searched his room for a shotgun shell. There had been no reason to, not until now. Clearly, I would have to go over there again.

For once, I found myself the only one home. Harry would be in about five-thirty; Hal had apparently come and gone, because the remains of a peanut butter and jelly sandwich orgy were on the counter; and there was no telling when Becky would wander in.

I cleared away the peanut butter and jelly and tried to think about supper. I thought taco bean salad might be nice, but to have taco bean salad today I had to have started it yesterday, which I couldn't quite manage. Spaghetti? No, I wasn't in a spaghetti mood.

Maybe we should go to Daniels. Or to Luby's. If it weren't for Daniels and Luby's I would have to prepare three hundred and sixty-five suppers a year, and my imagination isn't up to it.

Maybe if I didn't smell like Olead's cell I would feel more like thinking about what to cook for supper. That thought made me feel guilty and selfish again. He had to eat in it and sleep in it.

But there was nothing I could do about that now. Be logical, Deb, I told myself, and went and took a bath and washed my hair.

By the time I was out of the shower I had decided the heck with it, I'd make chili and rice and a salad, and anybody who didn't like that could sup on peanut butter.

Harry came home at a quarter to six and announced that he had to go help out at bingo because there was somebody out of town, and I asked if they weren't ever going to get back. He told me that the person who was gone was back, but now there was somebody else gone.

"Oh," I said, and started opening a can of chili. I am very fond of Harry, and I like the lodge just fine, but bingo I can do without.

"Do you want to come out with me?" he asked.

"No," I said. "Harry, I'm sorry, but I really don't feel like bingo tonight. I'm tired. I have a headache. Besides, I just washed my hair and I don't want it to get full of smoke again."

"Okay," he shrugged. "Well, you came out Monday, anyway. When is supper?"

"About five minutes."

Becky came in. Her hair was extremely tousled, she had no lipstick on, and she smelled like a sewer. Harry looked at her, horrified. "What in the world happened to you?" he asked, fairly reasonably I thought, although I also thought the answer was quite obvious.

"I was visiting Olead," she said, "and his cell stinks." She was looking slightly pleased with herself. Not extremely, but slightly.

"What were you doing?" Harry asked. "Lying down in it? You'd have to be, to get that smell all over you."

"Well, yes," she said breezily, and headed for her room. She slammed the door shut.

Harry turned to me, looking even more horrified. "Does that jail allow conjugal visits?" he demanded. "Because if they do, somebody better let them know—"

"They don't," I interrupted, and explained about the isolation cell, and about keeping Olead away from the rest of the jail population. "Though I am surprised they let her in," I added. "And she had to sit on the floor. There's nowhere else to sit. My clothes smell just as bad when I've been up there."

"Sitting on the floor's ass," Harry said, "she's been *lying* on the floor, and did you see her *hair?*"

"Well, what do you expect?" I asked, pouring the instant rice into the boiling water. "They're that age."

"I didn't expect my daughter to get laid in a jail, for crying out loud," Harry said, and I told him I didn't think she had. I told him I thought Olead had better sense.

"Well, Becky sure as hell doesn't," Harry said, and I said I wasn't sure of that either. Personally, I thought she just wanted to shock us.

Hal came in, banging his bike against the garage door, and asked if he could go to the movies with Tony Pierce to see *E.T.* Harry asked if he had done his homework and he said he had, so we told him he could go to the movie. I asked him if he wanted any supper and he said no, he wasn't hungry.

"I wonder why?" Harry said, as Hal departed with great speed and my last five-dollar bill. "He's always hungry."

I said I thought it might have something to do with the half a loaf of bread he'd had after school with jelly and peanut butter.

Just then Vicky and Don showed up unexpectedly. They always show up unexpectedly, having apparently forgotten the existence of the telephone after they moved into the same apartment. Vicky got through the door, but I wasn't sure how. She sat down and said, "Ouch."

"I think ouch," I said. "When are you going to go to the hospital and stay a while?"

"Don't rush me," she said. "I'm not due till the beginning of March."

"I don't believe that," I said. "Nobody gets that big in seven months. Not unless they're having twins. Or triplets."

"Well, I *am* this big," she answered. "And the doctor still says I'm not due till March. Guess what Don's got?"

A year ago Vicky had married Donald Ross Howell III, and with that name he'd have to be an attorney. I mean, where else do you go with a name like that? He is much nicer than you'd expect somebody named Donald Ross Howell III to be, but all the same he is an attorney, and I accused Vicky of treason when she picked him out. Don pointed out that he'd like to get on the DA's staff, which would put him on my side, but it'll take a while. He hasn't been an attorney long, and I don't quite know what they're living on in the way of money, especially since Vicky had to quit her job.

"A hell of a big case, with a chance at a hell of a big fee," Don said, looking puzzled. "Only problem is, I don't know if I'm competent to handle it or not."

"What case is that?" I asked, having a hunch I knew and hoping I was wrong.

"Olead Baker," he said.

I wasn't wrong.

"He called me about an hour ago," Don went on. "Said his girlfriend had recommended me. I told him I've got just about no criminal experience, and he said that was okay. I sure would like to know who his girlfriend is."

I gestured in the direction of Becky's bedroom door, and Vicky said, "Oh, no! Mom, that's awful!"

"Well," Don said grimly, "if she wants her boyfriend to get off, he needs somebody smarter than me, or at least more experienced. We talked for about an hour. He told me he wouldn't consider an insanity plea, and he told me the evidence against him includes gunpowder residue on his hands."

"You got it," I said. "Did he also tell you who took the warrant?"

"You didn't," he said, looking sick, and then he said, "Oh, yes, you did. Oh, hell, I want off this case. I never did want on it to start with, and now I *know* I don't want on it."

"I told him to get Racehorse Haynes," I said.

"I don't think Racehorse Haynes could get him out of this," Don said. "I mean, you can't very well claim self-defense against a four-year-old. If he won't claim insanity, then why doesn't he just plead guilty?"

"How about if he didn't do it?" I asked.

"Oh, hell, Deb, give me a break," Don said. Then he added, "While I was at the jail he got them to get his door key out of his property. He gave it to me and told me his girlfriend would be asking me for it so she could clean the house. I was going to go by the police station tomorrow to find out if the house is ready to be released. I don't suppose you could just tell me?"

"I've got to have one more look at a couple of things," I said, "but then it'll be ready. But Becky has no business going over there by herself. She can't begin to imagine what it looks like."

"Any way you could take me over there?" Don asked hopefully. "I guess if he's going to insist on me defending him, it might help for me to have a look at the scene before it gets cleaned up."

"I suppose you and I can go on over tonight," I said. I might sleep better if I found that sixth shotgun shell.

"That sounds fine to me," Vicky said, "if you don't mind if I just lie here on the couch until you get back. Mom, you have the most comfortable couch." She lay back happily.

I went and knocked on Becky's door. "Don and I are going over to Olead's house," I said.

Her door popped open. "I need to go too," she said. "I told Olead I'd go clean it up."

"Becky," I began, feeling rather helpless.

"Oh, I know it's a mess," she said earnestly. "And he said I wasn't to try to move any furniture or stuff like that. But he was fretting about the mess it was left in, and I told him I could at least get the floors clean. He didn't want me to do it, but I said really it was all right, and then he said he guessed he'd feel better if it got done."

"Well, come on," I said resignedly, and grabbed my camera. I kept a briefcase-size crime scene kit in the trunk of my car, but the time I tried leaving my camera there I wound up with a two hundred dollar repair bill.

We took my car. It is a commonly held theory that attorneys, especially attorneys with names like Donald Ross Howell III, have very large cars. Well, they don't, not when they're fresh out of law school. What they have are very large bills. I was a little puzzled about how Don and Vicky intended to transport their prospective infant in a car that size. I also was a little puzzled about how Vicky got in the car, or out of it, once she was in.

Don didn't say anything when he got in beside me. Becky, who didn't seem to be speaking to me unless she had to, got in back. After a while Don said sort of formally, "I think maybe I should not discuss the case with you, at least not until I have discussed it more thoroughly with my client."

"That's fine with me," I said.

A while after that he said, "You won't take anything personally, will you?"

"Don't worry about it," I said. I thought about telling him I would take it very personally if he didn't get Olead acquitted, but then I thought, well, it might not be possible, and if it isn't he's going to feel terrible. There's no sense making it worse.

When we got to the house Don took off to wander around by himself. Becky looked pale when she saw the den floor. "Mom," she said, forgetting she wasn't speaking to me, "I didn't know it would look like that."

"Well, that's how it looks," I told her.

"But I thought—what are those *clumps*?"

"It's blood, Becky. It's all blood."

"But it's *black*. It looks like—like stacks of plastic."

"Blood gets that way when it dries, if there's a lot of it. Becky, if it upsets you, you don't have to do it. He'll understand."

"No, I told him I'd do it," she said stubbornly, and looked under the sink for soap. I told her I'd help her, and she had to think about it a while before she decided that would be all right.

She started scrubbing the blood off the floor, and I tried to see how much of it I could get off the recliner chair. Finally I said, "This is impossible; it's soaked into the stuffing. The chair is going to have to be discarded." Obviously, I thought; who in the world would ever want to sit in it again no matter how clean I got it?

A bell rang somewhere in the house, and Becky jumped and her face went white. "It's just the telephone," I told her, and answered it.

"Deb?" Of course, as we should have guessed, it was Olead. "I called your house and your other daughter said y'all had gone to my house. What are you doing? Becky's not really trying to clean it up, is she? I didn't want her to, but she just kept insisting."

"Yes, she is," I said. "Olead, this brown recliner, there's no way of cleaning it."

"Then junk it. Put it out for the trash—hell, you and Becky can't carry that. Don't worry about it. All I'm going to do with any of it is give it to Goodwill, anyway."

"Don can carry it."

"Where is Don?"

"Around somewhere," I said. "Who did you want to talk to? Becky, or Don, or me?"

"Mostly Don, right now, really." He hesitated; then, just as I started to call Don, he asked, "Did Becky comb her hair before she went home?"

"No," I said.

"Damn it, I told her to," he said, sounding upset. "I mean, look, I've got enough trouble without—"

"Don't worry about it," I told him. "I'll get Don on the phone."

I called to Don, and when he picked up a phone somewhere in another part of the house I left Becky scrubbing and took the camera to the back yard. There were flood lights that lit it up very thoroughly, and there was a swimming pool that must be very pleasant in the long, hot summers. There were trees, on the other side of the pool, and there were holes in the trees. Small ones. At about shoulder height on me.

After taking my photographs, I used my pocketknife to dig in the tree.

Buckshot.

The trajectory was obvious; I turned and looked back at the house, in the direction the shot had come from, and of course I was looking at Olead's bedroom window.

I walked back toward the window, looking for the screen, and found it at last directly under the window. No, nobody had pried it off. It had apparently been pushed off from the inside, and as nasty as the weather had been this week, any fingerprints that might have been there had been washed off.

Only, of course, there hadn't been any, because whoever knocked the screen off (and it was about a hundred percent sure it was Olead himself) had used his hand, or the barrel or butt of a shotgun, to press against the mesh of the screen, not against the aluminum frame.

But those were new holes in the tree. My theory was looking better all the time—a sixth shot—only who in the hell had he been firing at?

And could I find the empty and find out for sure which shotgun it came out of—only it had to be the Browning, because the bruise was distinct enough that it showed the Browning was the one Olead fired, and he couldn't have fired the shot we already knew came out of the Browning, could he?

But I'd have to prove it. I had to find the sixth empty.

I went in Olead's room and started looking.

There wasn't much of a place to look. This was about as antiseptic as a hospital room, and less inviting.

The gray carpet would easily show up a shotgun shell, whatever color it was. I got a flashlight and directed the beam under the bed, and under the dresser, and under the desk, and I did not find a shotgun shell.

Don came in and asked me what I was doing, and I said, "Police business, counselor," and he left. I heard him in a minute dragging the recliner chair outside.

That was ratty of me. Poor Don has a hell of a mother-in-law. And I wasn't even mad at him; I was just pissed off because there had to be a shotgun shell somewhere in there and I couldn't find it.

I went back to the den, where Becky was still scrubbing. She looked up. "Mom," she said, "do rich people have to live like this?"

"What do you mean?" I asked.

"Like this," she repeated, and wiped her forehead with the back of her arm. "A living room that nobody lived in. A den for the grown-ups, but Mom, where did the children play?"

"They must have played somewhere," I said.

"Well, there aren't any toys in here," she said.

"Probably they were just put away," I said. "She'd been having a party that night, don't forget."

Becky shook her head. "It doesn't matter how well you clean," she said, from her experience as a live-in baby-sitter last summer. "There's always something you miss. Some little piece of a toy or game always gets under something. Always. They didn't play in here. I'll bet they were just allowed in here to watch television. I'll bet they had to play in their rooms all the time. I'll bet—I'll bet they didn't play much. Do rich people have to live like this?"

"Of course not," I told her. "Rich people are just people with money. Some of them like their children and some of them don't, just like anybody else. These people weren't really rich, but even if they had been that wouldn't be the reason they didn't like their children—if they didn't," I added hastily, reminding myself I was jumping to conclusions on insufficient evidence.

She shook her head. "I like our house better," she said. "I mean, we yell a lot, and the house is always messy, but—it's like you said. We *like* each other. It's okay even if it is noisy."

"I'm glad you think so," I said, a little surprised by her philosophizing.

"Anyway," she added, "why did they have the children if they didn't like them?"

"Maybe they liked the idea of having them better than they liked the fact of having them," I suggested.

"Maybe," she said. "I'll bet they were mad when Olead came home."

"What makes you say that?"

"Oh, because he does things his way," she said vaguely. "He told me he didn't have to go home, after he got out of that clinic. He could have gone anywhere he wanted to. But he decided to go home because he wanted to try to get reacquainted with his mother, and because he wanted to get to know his brother and sister. And then he stayed because of the children, because he could pay attention to them, see to it they had a little fun. And so—he didn't exactly put it like this. But his mother kept on trying to treat him just like she did when he was fourteen, bossing him around and all that, and he said every time she got really unreasonable he'd think, 'I don't have to take this. I can leave if I want to. But I can't take the kids with me.' And then he'd go and do whatever it was she told him to, or not do whatever it was she told him not to do, and he'd remember that it was his choice, and that way he wouldn't get mad. But he'd always stop and think about it first, and that made her mad."

"That's interesting," I said.

"He said Jack hit him one time, when he was really mad. Hit him hard. He said he started to hit Jack back, but he decided not to. He went in his room until he cooled off. And then he went back in the den and he said, 'Jack, I took that because I chose to, not because I had to. But you won't ever do that again, because if you do one of us is moving out of this house, and I suggest you remember which one of us owns it.' And he didn't wait for Jack to answer; he just went back in his room, and then after a while he got up and went and took the trash out, which was what Jack had told him to do to start with. He'd have left eventually, of course. He told me he knew he couldn't wait until Jeffrey got in school, because he'd be thirty-one by then. But he could stick it out for a while, at least until he decided what he wanted to do with his life."

She stood up. "Does the floor look okay to you now?"

"It looks fine to me. Becky, there's not really anything we're going to be able to do about the bedroom. That square of carpet is going to have to be cut out and replaced."

"I know," she said. "But he wanted me to see if I could find Jeffrey's baby book. I—he wants me to keep it for him." She looked as if she wanted to cry, but she didn't. I wondered whether Olead had jumped on her about crying so much.

I showed the room to her and she said, rather inadequately, "Oh my gosh."

Don, behind us, apparently had decided to forgive me for snapping at him. "We can't leave it like this," he said. "If I move the furniture, we can get it back to looking something like decent."

It wasn't in nearly as bad a state as I had originally seen it. We had searched the room thoroughly, and the furniture was now in fairly orderly stacks where the patrolmen who had come to help me had left it. But certainly none of it was at all where it belonged.

With Don doing most of the heavy work, we got the

things that appeared to have come from the parents' bedroom back into it, and we got the king-size bed that had been in this bedroom back together. We got drawers back in, and things back in drawers. We could not, of course, do anything about the crib, which was beyond repair.

To me, the whole project was a total exercise in futility.

And we didn't find the baby book.

"It's got to be somewhere in the house," Becky said. "He told me he couldn't remember where he had it last." She went back into the big master bedroom, opening drawers with as much aplomb as if she had the right to do so—which I suppose she did, since Olead had given her permission to be here, and he owned the house.

A fact I had to keep reminding myself of.

A fact Jack obviously had not wanted to remember.

And that was interesting.

"Where's Olead's room?" Becky asked.

I showed her Olead's room and she entered it rather hesitantly. She had been in the rest of the house cleaning, looking for things, working. She clearly felt different here. This was Olead's own room; it was his private space, and she may have felt a little as if she were prying.

"He asked me to get him some more books, too," she said. "Mom, can you take them to him tomorrow? They won't let me visit every day."

"Sure," I said.

She opened the closet door; there was a box of books there, but Jeffrey's baby book wasn't in it. What was in it, apparently, was every textbook Olead had used all the way through college. She started sorting through them, and I stared, fascinated, at how different his handwriting had been from day to day depending, I supposed, on his condition at that particular time.

I couldn't imagine how he had managed to get through college, in the mental state he must have been in. To have worked around insanity and consistently heavy sedation and still made any sort of decent grades at all, he must be some sort of genius.

"I think these are the ones he wanted," she said, and put the box back in the closet.

Then she looked on the bookshelf above his desk, and on his desk, and in his desk drawers. The baby book was in one of them.

I opened it, glanced through it. Every entry for the last six months was in Olead's handwriting, his now consistently even and neat handwriting.

"I think while I'm here I'll change the sheets," Becky said, and I could hear wistfulness in her voice. It was a sort of magic to her, I thought suddenly: if I clean up his house, if I put fresh sheets on his bed, then of course he'll come home.

I wished the magic could work.

She found clean sheets; apparently he kept his bedding in his own room, on a closet shelf. She jerked the old top sheet off, and I heard a thunk as something hard hit the wall. "What in the world was that?" she asked, turning, and then she picked it up. "Mama, what is this?"

"It's a shotgun shell," I said. "An empty. It's what I've been looking for." It was, as I had guessed, a red paper Remington hull, matching the one found near Brenda's body. The old Browning we'd found in his room, that had to be where it came from. The shotgun that couldn't be traced because, like many very old shotguns, it had no serial number on it, the shotgun the killer had brought with him deliberately to implicate Olead, I was beginning to guess now, the shotgun that the killer had brought with him in the name of going hunting. It must have had the two old shells left in it, and the killer hadn't ejected them, he'd just loaded new shells on top of them, new shells that probably came out of Jack's box.

"Why were you looking for it?" Don asked.

"Because I knew it had to be here," I said. "Don't you understand? Don't either one of you understand?"

"No," Don said, and Becky shook her head.

"Look," I said, "there were five shots fired here that night that killed people. And Olead had gunpowder on his hands and a bruise on his shoulder from the butt of a shotgun. He definitely fired a shot that night, even though he doesn't remember it. But if he didn't fire a shot that killed someone, then he had to fire a shot that didn't. And if that was so, then there had to be a sixth empty somewhere. And there was. And you found it."

Don looked at it. He whistled. "Well, I'll be damned," he said.

"Oh, my goodness," Becky said limply.

And I said, 'Counselor, would you like to cross-examine?"

This time he didn't mind being called counselor. "Not now, officer, but just you wait. Just you wait till I've got you on the stand."

9

I was sitting at my desk the next morning trying to think about the Blackburn case, when the intercom rang. The receptionist said vaguely, "There's a Susan Brown to see you."

"Send her on back," I said resignedly. It was beginning to appear that I would never get to think about the Blackburn case.

My office is only about twenty feet from the receptionist's desk, which is in the hall directly in front of the elevators. I looked up seconds later to see a woman I supposed must be Susan Brown. She was about my age and plumper than I am, and her hair, grayer than mine, was coming unplaited from the two braids crossing the top of her head. She was wearing a pink angora sweater and a pink-and-gray plaid fringed skirt fastened at about knee-level with a large gold costume jewelry safety pin; her matching pink-and-gray fringed shawl was held together with a perfectly ordinary aluminum safety pin. She had completed the ensemble with a silver hieroglyphic pendant and brown cowboy boots. "I'm looking for D. N. Ralston," she said in a voice somewhat firmer than I would have expected from her appearance.

"I'm Deb Ralston," I told her. I supposed she had been

reading a warrant. I always sign my warrants with my initials. How can I expect a crook to be frightened of somebody named Debra?

She looked at me, seeming rather puzzled. "Deb Ralston," she repeated. "I expect you wanted to talk with me."

"Not that I know of," I said. "Susan Brown? I can't think what it would have been for."

"Susan Braun," she corrected, and spelled it.

"Oh," I said. "Olead's doctor."

"That's right."

"You don't look to me like a psychiatrist," I said lamely.

"You don't look to me like a cop," she answered, and we laughed together. She must have heard my words as often as I had heard hers.

"Sit down," I offered, and she sat.

"I want you to know," she said, with no sort of preliminary, "that there is no way on earth that Olead Baker could have committed that crime."

"I agree with you," I interrupted.

I wasn't sure she heard me. She went on, fiercely, as if by making me believe her she could halt the prosecution. "Olead has been in the care of the Braun Clinic for eleven years. Although I strenuously disagree with much of my father's methodology and many of his interpretations of behavior, I am confident of his ability to record facts. We have a file on that boy two feet thick. He has never displayed violence toward anyone, except for about four occasions when he unexpectedly went out of control and attacked whoever was closest. Even that has not happened in over seven years. Furthermore, he is well now. He could not—"

She stopped abruptly. "Is he getting his vitamins?"

"Yes, I'm seeing to that," I assured her.

She sighed. "Thank God for some favors. Under normal circumstances, I really don't think there would be much if any deterioration even without it, but the combination of abrupt deprivation and the stress he must now be under could be moderately harmful."

"He seemed to think if he missed five days he'd be back in the shape he was in eleven years ago," I said. "I didn't know—"

"It's possible, of course, but extremely doubtful. His last acute attack was when he was nineteen, and I really think he'd have been completely well years ago, if it hadn't been for—" She stopped abruptly and, for the first time, reacted to what I had said. "You agree with me? Then why is he locked up?"

"Because the DA's office doesn't agree with us," I said, and told her about the evidence.

"You mean he actually fired—" She paused, her eyes astonished. "Now I do wonder why! And that poor little girl—well, it's no wonder he's blanked it out, as much as he doted on her. . . . And an overdose of Mellaril. That doesn't make any sense at all. He hasn't had any Mellaril since, oh, since he was sixteen. It never did seem to help him much. I'm sure he never at any time took any of it home."

"That's interesting," I said, half to myself. "I wonder where it came from."

She glared at me. "But you took the warrant," she said accusingly. "If you think he's innocent, why—"

"I was ordered to. If I hadn't, I'd have been taken off the case. And if I'd been taken off the case I wouldn't have had a chance to do any more digging," I explained. "And I don't think anyone else would have worked to clear him."

"I'd like to see him," she said.

I called the jail.

The jail said Olead Baker could see his doctor, if I wanted to bring her over.

In honor of the doctor, they let us use the conference room. I had warned her on the way over what to expect, but all the same she closed her eyes momentarily when Olead was brought in. He had healed considerably, but it still was quite obvious that he'd been at the losing end of a one-sided fight; furthermore, his drab blue-gray jail coveralls smelled of the isolation cell, and his bare feet were not exactly suited to the January chill and the concrete floor.

His beard, on the other hand, was coming along nicely; I had about decided it was going to be auburn.

"Susan!" he said happily, and greeted her with a much more exuberant hug than I expected would have met his mother. "I thought you were still in Egypt!"

"No, I got home last night," she told him, "and I must say I wasn't exactly overjoyed by the news that met me."

His smile was gone. He sat down abruptly and reached for the vitamins and the diet Dr. Pepper I always brought him, swallowed, and thanked me absently. "Susan," he said then, "I didn't do it."

"Of course you didn't," she said indignantly. "What we need to do is to figure out how to prove it."

He didn't sigh, but his expression sighed for him. "Super," he said gloomily, "that makes two people who believe me, you and Becky."

Susan glanced at me, startled, and I asked, "What did you say?"

"I said—" He stared at me. "You don't, do you?"

"Of course I believe you!" I said, more sharply than I meant to. "Why on earth would you think I didn't?"

"You keep asking me to remember firing the shotgun—" He stopped, stared at me again. "I thought you meant—you keep saying *if* I didn't do it—"

I stood up and walked around the table to him. Standing behind him, I dropped my hands on his shoulders as I would have done if it were Hal in trouble, and I began to knead the taut muscles that betrayed the fear beneath his mask of calm acceptance. "Olead," I told him, "I want you to listen to me. I'm going to distinguish between what I know and what I surmise and what I guess. Don't worry about the 'if' because it's the only way I know to put things. I mean, if you are accused of something, either you did it or you didn't, and in this case if you didn't do it then somebody else did. That's all I've been saying, and I don't know any other way to say it. Now, you listen to me and hear what I say, not what you think I might mean, okay?"

"Okay," he said, sounding tired.

"I *know*," I told him, as gently as I could, "that you fired a shotgun that night." I felt the muscles jerk as he started to protest, and I said quickly, "No, you listen to me. The bruise on your shoulder and the gunpowder residue on your hands are physical evidence. They're *facts*, Olead, and they won't go away. Clearly you don't remember doing it, but you did fire a shotgun that night."

"But—"

"*Listen*," I said firmly, and went on. "Now, from the fact that the screen was out, and the fact that Becky found an old red paper empty in your bed—"

"*Becky* found—"

"You hush. Yes, Becky found it. And from those facts, and the location of the shot pattern in the back yard, I *deduce* that you knocked the screen out, possibly with the barrel of the shotgun, and fired out the back window. I deduce that because I know that you fired one of the two shots that was fired with that old Browning, and I know that the killer fired the other."

I felt him relax when I said that.

"What I *think*," I went on, "is that you somehow got the Browning, the one in the room, away from the killer. I don't think it was your father's gun, by the way; I think the killer brought it with him. I think you got the gun and he went out the patio door and you shot at him and then for some reason immediately blanked out the whole thing."

"That is possible, Olead," Susan said. She had been listening intently. "Even people who've never had any kind of mental problems blank out that type of thing quite readily, as a result of the emotional trauma."

Olead shook his head. "I've never fired a gun in my life," he said firmly, "and nobody's going to make me say I did."

"Let me see your shoulder," Susan said quietly.

Olead looked at her, his jaw taking on that very stubborn set I had already seen on him a few times earlier. Then, his expression defiant, he yanked at the collar of the coveralls. Snaps popped open, and he slid the cloth off his right shoulder. "That ident tech, what's his name, already came over here today and took a picture of it," he said angrily. "He's been doing it every day."

"And this'll be about the most impressive," Susan answered, looking at the bruise. "It'll be starting to fade in a day or two. Olead, have you looked at it yourself?"

"I don't need to look at it," he argued. "I can feel it. Ouch!"

Susan, who had touched the bruise experimentally, looked at him with a rather startled expression, and he grinned ruefully. "Well, it's a little sore," he said defensively, and then grinned again. "Okay, I was putting on. But it really is a little sore."

"I expect it's a lot sore," Susan answered. "Olead, if you didn't fire a shotgun, how did that mark get on your shoulder? Look, you can make out the checkerboard effect of the stock—what's that called?" she asked me.

"Checkering," I said, "and you don't usually find it on the end of the stock. That's another reason I'm sure it was the Browning he fired; it did have checkering there, and it looked hand-carved. Come to think of it, I'll bet the lab will be able to look at a photograph of that bruise, the way it looks today, and make a positive identification, as irregular as that hand-checkering is."

"That's just what I need," Olead said bitterly.

Susan sat down again. "Well," she said, "if you didn't fire a shotgun how did you get the mark of the gun butt on your shoulder and gunpowder residue on your hands?" She looked at him expectantly.

He shrugged the coveralls back on and began to snap them, turning his back to her. "I don't know," he said sullenly. "How am I supposed to know?"

"You're the one who's so sure Deb is wrong," she said. "So I thought you might have some other explanation."

"Well, I don't, and you didn't think I did anyhow." He swung around to face her. "Did you?"

"No, not really."

"Then what do you think? You agree with Deb, don't you? You think I fired a shotgun and forgot about it? You think I'm that crazy?"

"Olead, you're well. I don't know how many times I've told you that. And what I think is that firing a shotgun is tied up with some other memories so painful you can't stand to remember them, and so you've repressed that memory along with the others. And that doesn't say a thing about your sanity. People do it all the time. It's often a way of preserving sanity."

He turned again, to face the mirrored glass that surrounded the room, and I wondered if he knew it was mirrored only from the inside. From the outside, the bewildered anger in his face must have been as evident as his clenched fist, and I wasn't surprised when a jailer knocked on the door to ask if everything was all right in there. I told him everything was fine in here.

Then I said, "Olead, there is a way of finding out. As Susan told you, this is something that often happens, and the police often have to get at the buried memories. We have something called forensic hypnosis—"

That was as far as he let me get. "Uh-uh," he interrupted. "No way. Not no but hell no. No cop is messing around with my mind."

"It won't—" I began.

"I said *no!*" he shouted.

I stood up. "Would you like me to leave and let you talk with your doctor?" I asked. Without waiting for an answer, I headed for the door.

"Deb?" His voice stopped me. "You don't have to go. I don't think I have any secrets." He took a deep breath. "Susan," he said, "you've hypnotized me before. I don't guess I'd be scared for you to."

After some more discussion, we finally decided to go back to Olead's cell where he could relax, and after Susan hypnotized him I would ask questions. All of which made me feel vaguely like something out of a Charlie Chan movie, because that's certainly not the way forensic hypnosis is normally done.

As I could have predicted, Susan was utterly horrified at the cell. "Look," she said, "we have padded cells in my clinic. We have to have them, sometimes. But they don't have to smell like this."

I told her that sometimes the cell was used for drunks, and they tend to vomit. Among other things. She replied, with some acerbity, "And sometimes the mentally ill wind up doing all of those things, including rolling on the floor in their own feces. But the floor gets cleaned up when they're through."

Olead cleared his throat. "As one who knows, having been in all the cells in question," he said, "let me get a word in edgewise. I've scrubbed the floor and walls in here myself, twice with pine oil and once with Clorox. You can't get the smell out. I tried. It's soaked in some way. The only way to get rid of it would be to burn the padding and start over. And if they were going to do that they'd have to stick me back in a regular cell while they were doing it, and I'm afraid that comes under the heading of thanks but no thanks. I'd rather stink than get beat up again. Can we get on with this?"

Susan must have hypnotized him several times in the past, because quite obviously he wasn't afraid of being hypnotized by her. It only took about three minutes. Then he was sitting quietly, leaning back against the back wall of the cell, with his legs stretched out in front of him, his eyes closed, and his face relaxed. I hadn't realized how much his features mirrored his tension, until for the first time I saw him without that tension.

Susan moved back, and I took her place. I was thinking fast; what did I need to cover? We should have planned for this. I should have made notes. Let's see, the party. Who was at it; especially, who gave him the punch? And the shots, did he hear any of them? And most important, when and why did he fire a gun himself?

"Olead," I said, "I'm going to ask you some questions now. Is that okay?"

"Yes," he said. He didn't sound asleep. He sounded drowsy, relaxed, but reasonably alert.

"Do you remember the New Year's Eve party?"

"Yes."

"Who came to it?"

"Friends of Mother. Friends of Jack. I don't know their names. Jake was there. Edith wasn't. She was in bed."

"You had a cup of punch. Who gave it to you?"

"A man."

"What man?"

"A man. He had a mustache. He told me he knew my daddy. But I don't know him."

Susan leaned forward. "Olead, you're at that party," she said. "We need you to tell me what you see. Does the man say anything else?"

"Says he might go hunting with Jack."

"Is he a nice man?" I asked, not sure why I was asking.

But that got a reaction. "No!" Olead said violently. "He pretends to like me, but he doesn't like me. His eyes are like a pig's eyes. He has mean little eyes. I want him to go away."

"Does he?"

"No. He stayed. I went to bed, but he stayed. He didn't go away." He was back in the past tense again. I looked at Susan. She shrugged. "Sometimes people won't stay in the present," she said softly. "Let it go."

"After you went to bed, did anything happen to disturb you?" I asked.

"Like what?"

"Like a loud sound. Do you remember hearing anything?"

"Loud noise," he said. "Outside my room. But it was okay."

"How did you know it was okay."

"He said it was okay."

"Who said it was okay?"

"Man."

"What man?"

His head turned from side to side; sweat was breaking out on his face. "He said it was okay," he repeated. "Then he came in my room. He went in my closet. I asked him why. He said he had to put some things away."

"What things?"

"Some things."

"Who was he?"

"Man."

"What man? What did he look like?"

"He said it was okay."

We were going in circles. This memory was blocked; something in him didn't want it to get out.

"Did anything else happen?"

"He sat on my bed. No! I don't want—" He turned his head again, vomited on his shoulder, and woke up.

A guard took Olead to get a shower, and I heard yelling in the halls as he went by. He was right; he wouldn't be safe returned to the general jail population. A runaround came in with pine oil and cleaned the cell, and Susan said, "Damn, he's lost his vitamins. Why do you have to bring them to him anyway? Why can't the jail just let him have them?"

"They won't let any prisoner have any kind of medication unless it comes in a prescription bottle with a label."

"Then I'll take care of that," she said. "I'll get them over here tonight and they can start giving them to him right away, since what you gave him didn't stay down long enough to do any good."

"I wonder why he did that?" I asked.

"He's blocked the memory," Susan said gloomily. "We're not going to find out for a while. Whatever it is, it's something he can't handle even in the upper part of his subconscious yet. It must be damn bad, because he's tough—tougher than you're likely to realize, just seeing him as he is right now. All that's been wrong with him for the last year has been a need to finish growing up, and I think he's about done that now."

"Susan, what—really—did he have?" I asked. "I mean, I always thought schizophrenia was about incurable. Look, was he really schizophrenic or not?"

"Schizophrenia's a label," Susan answered. "And in his case it may or may not be an accurate label. Deb, what he had—and never mind labels—acted like schizophrenia, but it was complicated by his home situation, which was a lot worse than he remembers it as being. Most of the time—not all the time, but most of the time—he was functioning normally at the clinic. Send him home and he'd go acute. My father decided, from that, that he was completely schizophrenic. And he wasn't. He never was."

"You're saying he was misdiagnosed? Then why—"

She interrupted again. "That's not exactly what I'm saying either. Definitions change. Schizophrenia used to be sort of a catchall diagnosis. My father went to medical school over fifty years ago, and he didn't really keep up with later developments. And Olead is tough. He wasn't always, but he is now. His mother bullied him. His father bullied him— in the kindest possible way, but it was still bullying. *My* father bullied him. And he didn't know how to fight back, so he—escaped. He escaped into his mind. And then when he started to learn how to fight back instead of escaping, my father saw it not as a healing but as symptomatic. Olead quit taking oral sedatives—he started flushing them instead of swallowing them—and he got caught when the toilet overflowed. So he got injections instead. There were more situations like that. He spent the last six years or so that my father was alive resisting being bullied, getting stronger and stronger, and my father—I hate to admit it, but my father was a lousy doctor and he was never board-certified as a psychiatrist—he never saw what was happening. He just kept writing on the charts that the patient was resistant to therapy. Of course Olead was resistant to therapy! He didn't *need* therapy—at least not that sort! I can't tell you for sure that he was never schizophrenic, because the more we find out about schizophrenia the more we know we don't know. But I don't think he ever was."

"Then why all the vitamins? And the panic about his not getting them?"

"He did respond to the B vitamins. Remember, he'd been under sedation for most of eleven years, and that alone would have him utterly depleted of any water-soluble vitamin. And *if* he was mildly schizophrenic, which I can't completely rule out as a possibility, then the vitamins *might* be making a difference. I'm afraid to risk pulling him off them. Now, especially."

"But look, if all that's true," I demanded, "then why does *he* think—"

Susan was getting bad about interrupting. "I guess because he hasn't really taken in what I've told him. He's afraid to believe me. He's spent eleven years being told he's incurably insane. Now I'm trying to tell him he isn't and never was. If you were him, how easy would you find to believe it?"

I didn't have time to answer, because Olead reentered the cell, clean, his hair and beard wet and curling. He was in a new set of jail coveralls that was quite indistinguishable from the old set. He looked down at Susan and me, sitting side by side on the floor, and we looked up at him. "Don't close the door," Susan called to the guard. "I have to leave." She began to get up.

"Why?" Olead asked.

"Got to get you some more vitamins," she told him, and he asked her to come back later.

Then he sat down beside me. "That didn't help much, did it?" he asked.

"I think I know now who did it," I told him. "But I don't know who he was."

"I think you'd better translate that."

"I think it was a man at the party," I explained. "You said he gave you the punch. And the best that I can figure out, the punch is the only chance anybody had to drug you."

"Is there anything we've got yet going to do me any good?" he asked. "Please tell me the truth, Deb. You're the only one who really knows how bad it looks. Don doesn't, not yet, and I gather he won't be allowed to look at the case file."

He didn't want a soothing lie. "It looks just about as bad as possible, Olead. If—if I wanted a conviction, I'd be saying I had a real good case."

"I see," he said. He got up, paced back and forth a minute or two, and then sat back down across from me. "I wonder what a lethal injection feels like," he said.

"Oh, God," I said, and it wasn't profanity. We were both silent for a while.

"You keep talking about four shots in the den," Olead commented finally, sitting apparently comfortably on the cell floor, leaning back on the side wall with his long legs stretched out in front of him. "Wouldn't there have been *five*?"

"Why five?" I asked. "Five in the house besides the extra, yes, but only four in the den." I was in approximately the same position he was, leaning back against the opposite wall facing him, but I could not so easily forget the stench of the cell, and I was far less comfortable than he appeared to be.

"Well, the cat," he said, and I shook my head. "Why not the cat?" he asked then. "What did happen to the cat?"

I shook my head again. That was so utterly nasty I didn't want to discuss it, although I knew it would come out in court. And the awful thing was it pointed to Olead in several ways, because psychologists have found that when a pet is killed during a mass murder of the family, it is almost always a family member doing the killing because to an outsider the pet is an animal, but to the family member it is part of the family he is trying to destroy.

"I remember when Brenda brought that cat home," he commented, breaking into my thought. "It was July; I'd just been home about a month. Brenda had been talking about getting a cat and Mother kept shushing her, and it didn't even occur to me she was thinking—well, I guess you know that when I was nuts I'd take my clothes off every time I saw a cat. Don't exactly know why; I know I was scared of them, but I don't know what that had to do with taking my clothes off. Well—Mother—never really believed I was well. And I guess she was afraid a cat would flip me out again. So Brenda apparently decided she was tired of arguing. I was out on the patio by the pool—I'd been swimming and was about tired out, and I had come out of the water and I was lying in a lounge chair sunning, which I can't do much of because I blister easy."

That explained his lack of tan. And I didn't think I would ever get used to hearing him calmly say such things as "when I was nuts." But he was smiling slightly and still talking.

"Anyhow, Brenda walked in the back patio gate lugging this big old white Persian cat, so old it looked a little rusty, and she announced, 'Marcy gave it to me. She got allergic to it.' And she marched up to me, with that cat looking about as big as she was, and you know what? I looked at it, and I was scared—I think if anybody had a blood-pressure cuff on me about then the results would have been alarming. But I made myself sit still—couldn't let Brenda see big brother run away from a cat, for God's sake. I sat there breaking out in a cold sweat and watching her walk up to me with the thing, and I looked at it, and I thought, 'What in the hell am I scared of?' It had—four rather useless-looking feet, and a whole lot of rusty white fur, and green eyes, and a silly flat face, and when she petted it, it made this kinda funny whirring noise, and I asked myself, 'What in the hell are you scared of, turkey?' I reached out and touched its ear and it said 'Mew.' That's about the silliest sound I ever heard in my life, mew. I think the cat that scared me to start with must have been a Siamese, you know how they sound, *rrooow*, like a jet plane taking off, but this said mew. Very softly and delicately. And I laughed."

He was laughing now, remembering. "I thought, I'll be damned, it's just a kinda funny little animal, that's all. And all I was scared of was just the memory of being so scared before. And then she dumped it in my lap and marched off, and it turned around a couple of times and then I guess it decided it would take too much energy to leave, so it would just go to sleep instead. So it did, on my knees, just a blob of slightly wiggly fur, and I started petting it and it started making that funny whirring noise again. Okay—I know that's purring, but you got to admit, it's a funny whirring noise. It sounded rusty. I wanted to call the cat Rusty but I was out-voted."

I agreed that it was a funny whirring noise, although I had never thought about it that way before.

"And you know what?" he continued. "It felt good. It felt damn good, to touch it, to have that fur on my legs, and right then I had one of those—insights—you're supposed to get out of working with a shrink, only I never did." He looked at me. "Can I tell you about that?"

"You can tell me whatever you want to," I said.

He grinned affectionately. "Yeah, you're that kind of person, aren't you? Well, I remember—when I first started going nuts, before the first time I flipped out—I knew there was something wrong. I knew there was something bad wrong. I tried to tell Mother—I was seeing all this stuff, things would be big and little at the same time, and moving fast and slow at the same time, and near and far away at the same time—all right, I know that doesn't make sense, because it doesn't make much sense to me now, but it's the only way I know to describe it. And of course I kept running into things, because I didn't know what size they were, or how near they were, and I had so many near misses I had to stop riding my bike completely, because I couldn't judge speed or distance at all, and I kept throwing up because I was so dizzy from everything around me moving around all the time, and it scared me—and when I tried to tell Mother she told me, quite briskly, that was impossible. Well, of *course* it was impossible, and I knew perfectly well it was impossible, and that was exactly what was scaring me."

He shook his head. "I know she wasn't a shrink. But you'd think she'd have realized that when a fourteen- or fif-teen-year-old boy starts crying all the time there's something wrong."

I agreed. If Hal started crying all the time, I'd have him to the doctor fast.

"But all she kept telling me was to snap out of it. And I didn't know how to. I would have if I could have. Anyhow, it got to where the only thing I was pretty sure was staying the same was my own body, and if I had my eyes open I wasn't even sure it was. So I spent a lot of time in my room with my eyes closed holding onto myself so things would be still, and even with my eyes closed I was hallucinating—things that were taking huge steps toward me and covering the ground so fast and at the same time nothing was moving at all—damn it, I *know* it doesn't make sense!" he said savagely.

"It sounds terrifying," I answered.

"It was. It was. And so—look, you try to block it out any way you can, you know? And so—" His eyes were closed now; he was a little pale. Clearly, this memory was still distressing. "So—of course, as you can probably guess, Mother walked in one day when I was jacking off. And she was horrified. She let me know that in no uncertain terms. I think Dad tried to tell her it was okay. But she was convinced I was going to be a pervert. Better to be insane than a pervert. Anyhow, I think somehow I got it into my head that it must be bad to do anything that felt good. For about a year after I got to the clinic I wouldn't even take a bath unless somebody forced me to, because it felt good, so it must be bad."

He opened his eyes. "I'm not saying that was Mother's fault. I was already bad flaky by the time that happened; if I wasn't it probably wouldn't have upset me so much. But— maybe that was why I was scared of cats. They walk right up to you and rub their fur against your legs and make you feel good, so they must be really awful, you know? So—anyhow—there I was with the cat in my lap, and of course it was covering up my swim suit so you couldn't tell I had one on, and Mother walked out on the patio and the cat and I were both asleep. She woke us both up. Screaming."

He laughed. "So the cat dug its claws in and jumped off me and I jumped up and said, 'What's the matter?' and she said, 'Oh, Jimmy, you scared me!' And she was—she was so pale, I mean she was really white, and then I realized what she was scared of. And I said, 'No, I'm okay, but you've sure scared the hell out of Brenda's new cat.' I didn't even remind her I don't like being called Jimmy; she was too shook up. And then I went over and picked up the cat and took it in the house."

"Was she glad?" I asked.

"Glad?" he said. "I don't know. I know she was glad I didn't embarrass her again." He smiled again, very slightly. "Becky's hair is soft. Becky—" He didn't finish that sentence. "I was a little aggravated at her last night," he said, more briskly. "Because she told me she wasn't going to comb her hair, and I said, 'What do you think your parents are going to think when you go home looking like that?' and she said, 'I don't care. I hope they do!' So—just in case you wondered—we didn't. I wouldn't. Not here. I wanted to, a lot, and I think she did too, but we didn't."

"I really didn't think you did," I said.

"You don't want me to talk about that, do you?" he guessed. "Never mind. I won't any more. I just wanted you to know. What happened to the cat, Deb? Somebody's going to have to tell me, sooner or later."

I shuddered. "Somebody stomped it to death," I said reluctantly.

"Good grief," he said. "So I'm supposed to have done it because everybody knows, ol' Olead, he just don't like cats *noway*. The janitor at the clinic used to say that," he explained parenthetically. "This I'm supposed to have done barefooted?"

"No, there were shoe marks," I said.

"And of course nobody thought to look at any of my shoes to see if there was blood and cat hair on them?"

"We looked."

"Well?" he said finally.

"On your baseball shoes," I said, not wanting to say it.

"On my *baseball* shoes?" he repeated incredulously. And then, to my astonishment, he began to laugh softly. "On my baseball shoes! Deb, Deb, Deb, the bastard has made a mistake, the bastard has screwed up." He lifted one leg and wiggled his toes at me. "Size ten and a half," he said. "That's how big my feet are now. But those baseball shoes—let's see—they're going to be about size eight, because that's how big my feet were when I went away. Those baseball shoes were in my room for only one reason. They were wrapped up in my sleeping bag when I got it down to give to Brenda, and I hadn't gotten around to deciding whether to just stick them in the trash can or give them to Goodwill." Then his face sobered. "But I guess they'll say they were on my hands. Probably they were on the hands of whoever did it. And of course my fingerprints are on them, because I was handling them. But you know—I never did want to harm cats. I just wanted them to stay away from me. But I guess it'd take a shrink who worked with me then to say that, and he's dead. The bastard's dead. You know why I call him a bastard?"

"Why?"

"Because I don't know enough bad words," Olead said sorrowfully, and laughed at my astonished look. "No, because he read all that stuff about megavitamins. And he said it wouldn't work. Look, nobody ever said it would work all the time on all schizophrenia. It was a chance, that was all, but it was a chance that was worth trying, if nothing else was working. But he wouldn't let me try it. Then Susan went away to work at another clinic for a while and she *saw* it work and she came back and argued with him, and all he'd say was, no, it's just a fad—then I learned more about it in college, and I'd have walked over to a health food store and gotten them myself, only I was never allowed to carry money in case I decided to run away. Can you believe it?" He shook his head. "I could write a check for just about any amount of money you can name, if I could get my checkbook out of the old—man's—desk, but I couldn't get four dollars in cash to buy a bottle of niacinamide to put my head back together, if that was what I needed. So then I decided if he wouldn't give me what I wanted to take I'd quit taking what he wanted me to take. I had trouble sleeping for a while, but then I got where I could, and I felt *great*. I mean I really felt fine. But it was winter and the capsules, you know, they're gelatine and they didn't dissolve because the water was too cold, and the toilet got stopped up so he found out. So he started giving me shots. So I started taking the pills again. No sense getting shots. Even Susan says he was wrong. She told me I had a good case for malpractice if I wanted to pursue it, but what good would that do? It's not her fault, and the clinic is hers now. He's dead. But he was so darn stubborn, Deb, he thought he knew everything and I'll bet he hadn't read a medical journal in forty years. What it amounts to is eleven years of my life down the tubes because of one stubborn old man. And that hurts. That hurts like hell."

He wasn't looking at me, as he went on. "One time I read about an experiment and I went and told him about it. It was about some spiders. They extracted a substance from the blood of schizophrenic humans and injected it into spiders, and the spiders went crazy—in effect, they started spinning schizophrenic spiderwebs. So I asked him if he thought the spiders had my mother. He said I was being resistant to therapy. We wound up in a shouting match. You know what I got out of it? Shock treatment. That's all. Just shock treatment."

He looked at me then and my horror must have shown on my face, because he laughed again, very softly. "You've been watching too many late-night movies," he said. "It doesn't hurt and sometimes it helps break somebody out of an acute phase, especially if they're, you know, like real depressed or suicidal. It's just that it's a hell of a way to end an argument." He shivered. "You know what I'm scared of?"

"No, what are you scared of?"

"Not of dying," he said. "Not much. It can't be any worse than some of the places I've already been. No, what I'm scared of is that I'll get scared, that I won't at the last minute have the guts to walk into that room by myself, that

I'll make somebody have to carry me, or something. And I would like to die with some sort of dignity."

"Olead," I told him, "my husband said last night that from what he's heard of you he thinks you've got enough guts for a whole army to run on."

He looked pleased. "But I might run out of it," he said. "Deb—this is a hell of a thing to ask anybody. But I feel like I could make it, if you were there."

"Olead, I don't think you'd be able to see me."

"No, maybe not, but if I knew you were there—I'd be able to hold myself together, for you, even if I couldn't for me." He shook his head. "Forget it. I shouldn't have even brought it up. You don't ask somebody to come and watch you die."

"Nonsense," I managed to answer briskly. "People ask that every day. People who expect to die want their whole family to gather around them. It's not that much different."

"It is too and you know it," he said flatly. "Then you would, Deb?"

"I hope it never happens," I said. "But if it does and you want me, yes, I'll be there."

After a while he said thoughtfully, "If I can hack this I ought to be able to hack medical school, if I ever get a chance. What do you think?"

I told him I thought he'd make a very fine doctor, and he said, "If I don't get convicted—if I get a chance—if I get into medical school—I think I'll be a psychiatrist. A children's psychiatrist, maybe. I'll go back and work at Braun Clinic. I'd like that a lot, if I ever get a chance. And if a frog had wings—oh, hell, Deb, you have to go back to work."

10

It occurred to me after I got back to my office that with all the digging and questioning I was doing, I was getting no motive at all for anybody to kill Jack or Marilyn Carson. What I was getting, over and over again, was a motive for Jack Carson to want to murder Olead Baker.

He had been sitting pretty, that crop-duster pilot, married to a woman whose crazy son had four million dollars. He was living in a two-hundred-thousand-dollar house that crazy son had paid for, and I felt fairly certain that of the two Lincolns and the old Ford pickup around the house, the only one Jack had paid for was the pickup. And I wasn't even sure of that. I wondered how many other things Olead had casually written checks for because his mother wanted them, his mother who, according to him, loved him but didn't like him, his mother who was glad he hadn't embarrassed her again.

It must have been quite a shock to Jack when Olead got well. But even then Olead worked around the house, looked after the children, allowed himself to be bullied. How had Jack felt, when Olead reminded him of whose house that really was? And how long ago had that been?

A very unpleasant thought was beginning to wander

into my mind. Suppose I had the scenario all wrong? Suppose that man Olead remembered, the man who'd given him the punch, had been working with Jack? Suppose they had worked together to get rid of the others, to frame Olead? The plan might have been for it to look as if it had happened after Jack left for the hunting trip. Maybe he was going to say Jake changed his mind, decided not to go, decided to stay home with his sick wife, and then Olead flipped out. So easy, and Jack was rid of a wife he might be getting tired of. Edith, of course, was a pain anyway, and Jake? Jake was a completely unknown factor; I had no idea at all what he'd been like. He was Jack's brother, and he lived in Arkansas, and he liked to hunt rabbits on New Year's Day; that was all I knew about Jake Carson.

If that was the plan, leaving Jeffrey alive made perfect sense. If Olead was convicted, if he was executed for murder, then Jeffrey was his only living relative. But if he was acquitted on grounds of insanity, well, he loved Jeffrey. He'd see to it Jeffrey was provided for. And either way, Jack as Jeffrey's father continued to get all the nice perks he'd gotten used to, without the exasperating presence of a grown-up, no longer tractable, Olead Baker.

Suppose that was the plan, and it had started to work, and Jack and his friend were just congratulating themselves on their success when Olead woke up? Woke up and saw the shotgun they'd used to kill Brenda, realized what had happened, grabbed a shotgun, fired one shot at Jack, sitting in the living room, and killed him, and fired a second shot at Jack's friend as he fled?

Yes, I was sure which shotgun he had fired, and I was sure two shots had been fired out of it—but no firearms examiner in the world could tell me which load of shot came out of which shotgun. The best I could get was which empty shell was fired out of each shotgun, and I was guessing which shell had done what on the basis of which room the shells were found in. But empty shotgun shells are quite portable.

Could that be why he refused to remember, why he vomited when I demanded an answer?

Could Olead Baker have killed his stepfather?

If he had it probably wasn't murder; it probably was self-defense, because any man walking in on that kind of carnage could reasonably assume himself to be another prospective victim. But would a jury read it that way?

And again, could I prove it?

Somehow, I was going to have to do two things. First, I was going to have to locate some old friends of Olead's father, some people who had known Jim Baker and Jack Carson in the days when they were friends, before Carson stole Baker's wife.

Second, I was going to have to locate someone who had been at that party—preferably several someones who might be able to help one another remember who else had been there.

I could think of one way to work on the second. I called the *Star-Telegram*. And the television stations. And the radio stations. And Captain Millner was not going to be very happy about me. But soon every media outlet in the Metroplex was going to be asking any person who had been at a New Year's Eve party at Jack Carson's Ridglea house to call the Fort Worth Police Department.

It crossed my mind that maybe I'd better let dispatch know about that.

It was fortunate that I had, because several radio and television stations put it on the noon news, and by two o'clock I had nine people who had been at the party. Either they were all good citizens eager to cooperate, or else they were fantastically excited at the thought of having something to do with a real, honest-to-goodness *murder*, but at any rate they all produced names. The lists agreed and overlapped; no two people gave exactly the same list, but by the time I talked to all of them I had a fairly good idea who had been there.

And there was one name that interested me very much.

According to three people, Slade Blackburn had been at Jack and Marilyn Carson's party.

Oh, really, I thought.

Oh, that is nice.

Because I had shotgun shells, red paper Winchesters, at Slade Blackburn's house, but no shotgun. And I had a shotgun and two empty red paper Winchester shotgun shells at Jack Carson's house, which was really Olead Baker's house. And I had .45 ammunition, but no pistol, in the back of Jack Carson's truck, and I had no pistol at Slade Blackburn's house, but I did have a woman who had been shot to death with a .45, and I had a man who had definitely lied about everything he said had happened that day.

And the pistol was probably in the Trinity River. I didn't expect to find it.

Of course I couldn't arrest a man for being at a party. But I now had the two cases tied together, and I was feeling quite relieved. Olead will never even go to trial, I thought confidently; why, I'll bet I have him out by tomorrow. If the DA's office just hadn't insisted on running the warrant through when I hadn't completed my investigation, they wouldn't be embarrassed now by having to drop it. But since they did, well, that was just their problem.

This is so obvious, I thought. I'd call Olead, and he would tell me where he had his money deposited, and then I would call the federal bank examiners and the outside computer experts the FBI had called in to put together the burned paper records and the demolished computer tapes and disks from the bank, and I'd tell them what to look for, and then we would all go out and arrest Slade Blackburn.

How nice, how nice, I thought, confidently theorizing well ahead of my facts.

Blackburn must have thought it was simple: first get rid of Jack Carson who could have told on him, Jack Carson who had been sharing the loot. But he couldn't kill Olead—that would freeze his account, but getting rid of him this way wouldn't. And then the second stage in his plan, kill an aging, no longer attractive wife who didn't fit into his new life, and simultaneously fake a robbery in order to mask the destruction of the bank records that would otherwise show his guilt—that still would ultimately prove his guilt, I assured myself.

I called Olead and asked him how much money he had in the First Federated Bank of Ridglea, and he said, "None."

"What?" I said. "But surely—"

"I don't have any money in the First Federated Bank of Ridglea," he repeated.

"But Olead—"

"Deb," he interrupted, "I know where I do and don't have accounts, and I assure you I do not have an account of any kind in the First Federated Bank of Ridglea." He named off the banks where he had accounts.

"Are you sure?" I asked idiotically, and he said he was sure.

"Damn!" I said.

"Why?" he asked.

"Because I thought I had it all figured out," I said miserably. "Olead, do you remember a man—" I described Slade Blackburn.

"Where am I supposed to remember him from?"

"That party?" I asked hopefully.

"He might have been there," Olead said. "Deb, I just don't remember that party very well. I was in and out the first thirty minutes, because Jeffrey was a little cross and I was trying to get him settled down, and of course every time I went in there Edith acted like she thought I was going to rape her, hiding under the covers and hissing at me. And then after I finally got him asleep somebody handed me that cup of punch and then right after that I started getting sleepy. It's all blurry after that. I know I got the Dr. Pepper trying to wake up, and then I gave up and went to bed. By then I was so sleepy I was afraid I was going to fall over before I got my clothes off."

He had just told me how the killer knew not to harm

Jeffrey. And of course the killer hadn't known he cared just as much about Brenda because by then Brenda was already asleep.

"Could the man I described have been the person who gave you the punch?"

"Maybe," he said. "I'm sorry, but I don't translate verbal descriptions into mental pictures very well. That's just not my strong point. Show me a picture of him and maybe I'll know."

And I didn't dare do that. Because, if I was right, one day I was going to have Olead looking at Slade Blackburn in a lineup, and I couldn't risk doing anything that could be said later to have prejudiced Olead's memory.

So I hung up and contented myself with calling the bank and telling the bank examiners that if they found anything, anything at all, in the name of James Baker or James Olead Baker, they should examine it very thoroughly. They asked me if I had any grounds for the request, and I had to tell them that right now it was only a hunch.

Cops often play hunches.

But I had a hunch that bank examiners might like numbers better.

There was a dinner dance at the lodge that night, I reminded myself, noticing that I had once again managed to work well past quitting time. Harry would expect me to go and be a wife instead of a cop for the evening.

Maybe, I thought hopefully, maybe with that to take my mind off things, maybe I'd feel a lot better tomorrow.

Maybe.

Harry would expect me to have a new dress. Oh, my gosh, look at the time, I thought, and headed for Monnigs.

And then I headed for Dillards.

Once there, I decided that before I went to look at dresses I'd have enough time, if I rushed, to go have a quick peek at the baby clothes. After finding a cute little green romper suit I just couldn't resist, I remembered Hal needed new gym shorts and the washer had eaten Becky's favorite nightgown. Passing through the men's department on the way to ladies' dresses, I noticed they had an after-Christmas special on cufflinks. Good, I thought, because Harry certainly needed a new pair to go with his tuxedo. His old set just really hadn't been in good shape since the time he left them out on his dresser and the cat got them.

And driving gloves were on special. Good! I go through about two pairs every winter.

Laden with packages, I glanced at my watch again.

Well, maybe Harry wouldn't mind too much if I just wore a dress I already had, I told myself hopefully.

Fortunately he didn't, or else he didn't notice. He'd thrown a fit about my old dress after the Christmas dance and told me I had to get a new one; the fact that I refused to go to the store until after Christmas was a large part of the reason we didn't go to the New Year's dance.

Well, I promised myself, I'd get one before the Valentine's Day dance.

Harry got tired just as early as I did, unusual for him, and we got to bed before midnight. For the first time in a week I slept well, because I really felt I was on the right track, if I could just find some sort of a positive, provable link between Slade Blackburn and Jack Carson.

When I got up at eight, Hal was in the living room watching television by himself; he informed me that Becky had already left to go see Olead. Rather somnolently (having had a slight overdose of champagne the night before), I said something on the order of uh-huh and went in the kitchen to consider whether there was anything I could think of to make for breakfast that sounded interesting enough to be worth the trouble.

I had just put a pan of muffins in the oven when Becky returned. And she was crying. "What," I demanded, "is the matter with you?"

"Olead's not there!" she told me, somewhat dramatically.

"What in the world are you talking about?" I asked,

feeling not quite awake yet. "Of course he's there. Where else would he be?" I may have been thinking something to the effect that he better not have tried that walking act again.

Becky flung herself at the table, weeping, in an effect I think she got from a late-night movie. But there was no doubt that her distress was genuine. "I don't know!" she wailed. "They won't tell me! All they'll say is that he's been transferred!"

Of course he hadn't taken a walk again; I'd long since realized that his apparent dopiness the first day and part of the second was the combined result of shock and an overdose of Mellaril. "Well, hush up," I told her. "I'll find out."

I telephoned the jail and asked a few questions, pointing out (reasonably, I think) that Olead was my prisoner even if he had been transferred to the county, and that in view of the fact that my investigation was far from complete even if the DA's office had seen fit to take warrants I considered premature, I felt I did have a right to know where he was. Reluctantly, someone parted with the information that sometime late yesterday evening he had, per court order, been transferred to Terrell State Mental Hospital for ten days of testing and observation.

Ten days, I thought. How nice. That's the same length of time for testing and observation that a mad dog gets.

I asked why and was told that the DA's office had gotten word that Olead's psychiatrist had been up at the jail. As this gave the state even more reason to expect an insanity plea, the decision was reached to counter with tests by the state's own psychiatrists.

That was standard operating procedure; I had no problem with it. It seemed entirely reasonable. Except—

"Was he allowed to take his medication with him?"

"Oh, come on, Deb," the jailer protested. "Terrell's a hospital. Don't you suppose they'll have everything he needs?"

"Does that mean no, he wasn't?" I asked.

Well, yes, that was sort of what was meant.

Sort of.

"Thank you," I said, and hung up the phone and called Don. And then I called Susan, and while I was talking with Susan, Don was talking with a judge. Then Don called Susan, and then he called me back to say that he and Susan would be on their way to Terrell with a court order commanding that Olead be allowed to continue the course of medication prescribed for him by his personal physician. And Susan was taking new prescription bottles and copies of all her credentials, just in case there was some sort of question.

Becky said she wanted to go. I agreed that I did, too, but I pointed out that there was no earthly reason for us to. Besides that, I had muffins in the oven.

I reminded Becky that he'd probably be better off there. Most likely he'd have a lot more room to move around, and he'd be removed from the people who showed a continuing desire to beat him up. Besides, the testing would give him something to do, so he wouldn't be so bored.

And if we were lucky, I'd have the real killer in jail by the time Olead got back to Fort Worth.

Becky said that wasn't fair, and I agreed that the whole thing wasn't fair, but there didn't seem to be anything more we could do about it than what we were already doing. I then told Hal to be sure his dirty socks were all in the laundry hamper, because I wasn't searching any rooms without a search warrant, and he said, "Oh, Mom!" in a rather disgusted tone of voice.

"You, too, Becky," I added. "Either that or do your own laundry."

Harry wandered out of the bedroom yawning and asked whether he had smelled muffins and I told him yes. He said good, because he wasn't sure whether it was muffins or pinto beans, and he didn't really think he wanted pinto beans for breakfast. I told him the pinto beans were for a taco bean salad tomorrow, and he said something on the order of oh and added that he thought he was going to go look at a plane today. He asked if I wanted to go along. I told him I'd think about it. He said that wasn't until late this afternoon, so I had plenty of time to get the laundry done.

That was just what I wanted, plenty of time to get the laundry done. Did I promise to love, honor, cherish, and wash the socks?

At one in the afternoon I found that Becky, having an unusually severe attack of ambition, had cleaned her room without being yelled at or nagged. "Maybe she's growing up," I said to Harry, and he said that it was about time. He was sitting in the middle of the living room floor with the vacuum cleaner taken apart all around him.

This made me feel really ready for company when Don wandered in with Susan. Susan wasn't dressed up today. That meant she had on turquoise knit slacks, a turquoise Western-embroidered cowboy shirt, and brown cowboy boots. I thought she looked as much like a psychiatrist in that as I did like a cop in my brown knit slacks, sweat shirt with Bell Helicopter-Textron printed on it, and blue sneakers. Susan walked around the vacuum cleaner and sat on the couch, and Don parked himself on the raised hearth to inform us that Olead was okay.

"What does that mean?" Becky asked suspiciously.

"It means that when we got there he was in the gym dribbling a basketball and practicing making baskets, with two psychiatrists sitting there watching him do it," Susan said and started to laugh. "They got him up this morning and asked him what he wanted to do, and he told them he wanted to play basketball. So they were watching him play basketball. To see if he did it sanely or not, I suppose."

"But his medication?"

Don shook his head. "He told us it was nice of us to come and bring the court order, but we didn't need to. Seems he'd already told them what he was getting and they'd said there was no problem with continuing it."

"You see, there's one thing we forgot," Susan said. "The

state wants him to be sane. So they're not going to risk rocking the boat. Anyway, as I said to start with, I don't really think it matters. He's well. Period. With what he's been going through, if he was ever going to snap again he'd already have done it, medicine or no medicine. There's no psychiatrist in the world that would call him anything but sane now."

Becky suddenly decided to go to her room. "What's the matter with her?" asked Harry, who had disentangled himself from the vacuum cleaner and sat down in his recliner chair.

"I suspect she remembered why the state wants him to be sane," Don answered, and added, "Damn it!" I pointed out that things were getting better, and Don gloomily said he hoped so.

He and Susan left after a cup of coffee, and Harry said thoughtfully, "I've really got to meet this guy."

"I'll do my best to get you the chance," I answered, "but darn it, I'm supposed to be working two cases right now. I need to do something else about Blackburn, and I've mostly been leaving that up to the feds."

When I'm unusually wound up in a case Harry tends to feel a little neglected, although most of the time he seems to enjoy my job about as much as I do—he has been heard to brag, or tease, or both—that he's the only man at Bell Helicopter who sleeps with police protection. But I couldn't blame him for being a little put out right now; this situation had the entire family in an uproar.

"Isn't there anybody else in your squad?" he asked now, in some annoyance.

"Sure," I said. "Six people, fourteen cases. The original idea of the major case squad was one person, one case, no interruption, but it never works out that way. And right now I've got Olead Baker and Slade Blackburn."

"Slade Blackburn," Harry repeated thoughtfully, the exasperation evaporating as fast as it had come. "That really startled me, you know? I've known him for twenty years—

always known he was a high-roller, of course, but I wouldn't have picked him to pull that kind of a shenanigan."

"You didn't tell me that before," I said. "Where do you know him from? He's not in the lodge, is he?"

Harry grinned cheerfully. "Well," he said, "you remember when I was stationed in Grand Prairie and six of us went in together to buy an airplane?"

"I remember." Well did I remember. It had not been the high point of our marriage. We had been about as able to afford one-sixth of an airplane as a whole airplane.

"Slade was one of that six, him and Jim Baker both," he explained, and grinned again, reminiscently. "We rented a hangar in Fort Worth from a little bitty private airstrip so close to Meacham we had to get clearance from the Meacham tower to get into our own landing pattern, and we all swore as soon as we had the money we'd get better facilities. And all of us who still fly are still hangaring there."

I knew that, of course. It was just that I had never known—or if I'd known, I did not remember—that Slade Blackburn was involved.

"Slade Blackburn has an airplane?" I asked.

"Well, yeah," Harry said, sounding a little puzzled.

"At the same airstrip you use?"

"Yeah."

"Then would he have something like a locker out there, where he'd store stuff?"

"Yeah," Harry said. "All six of us got lockers out there when we first got the plane, and all of us who are still flying still have the same ones. All of us who are still flying." He shook his head, a wry expression on his face. "I should say all of us who are still alive. There's two of the group dead now."

"Slade Blackburn has got a locker at an airport." I wanted to be sure I understood.

"Well, an airstrip."

"And he has an airplane—what kind? How far will it go?"

"It's a Beech, of course. And it'll go just about as far as he wants to take it, provided he refuels on schedule," Harry said maddeningly. He then laughed and added, "I'm sorry, hon, I really don't know his range. I'd guess he could go from here to, say, the west coast in two, maybe three, hops, but that's just a guesstimate. Ask me whatever you want to about *my* plane." Harry thinks Beech is the only kind of plane there is, except a Mooney, which is out of his price range, but he does admit that Cessna and Piper owners tend to feel the same way about Cessnas and Pipers.

And in fact, as he knows perfectly well, the only question I ever ask him about his plane is whether it will get us where we want to go. I fly in it gladly as long as Harry does not ask me to learn to do the piloting, although I did reluctantly learn to land it so that I could in an emergency. What I don't understand is Harry's mad passion to fly up in the air and fly about in circles and then land again. I regard airplanes as transportation. Harry regards aircraft of all types as toys.

"Is that where you're going to look at an airplane?" I asked. "That airstrip?"

"Yeah," he said. "I'm thinking about selling mine and maybe getting this one. But maybe not. I don't know."

I did not feel extremely alarmed by that statement. Harry has been flying the same plane for the last six years. At least once a month he goes and looks at a potential replacement, and each time he finally decides against it. I am never terribly excited about the prospect of going to look at another plane, although I usually go with him and dutifully admire every one, but the prospect of a look at Slade Blackburn's locker—now, that was another matter.

I told Harry I'd go with him, and he said, "Good, grab your jacket."

"Aren't you going to put the vacuum cleaner back together?" I asked.

He glanced at it. "Do it when I get home."

I hoped he would. Before and during taking it apart, he

had carefully removed the string, thread, carpet fibers, and other assorted dirt from it. And just as carefully deposited it all on the carpet. Hal, under suitable coercion, had removed the larger chunks and taken them to the trash can, but the carpet was still covered—I mean *covered*—with a fine, light sifting of gray dust.

When I think of a hangar, I think of a building. One with a door, one that can be locked. This airstrip allegedly hangars thirty assorted airplanes. In fact, twenty-three of them had no hangars at all; they were merely tied down, which meant that rope was tied through loops on various portions of the aircraft's anatomy (look, I'm not a pilot; I don't know what those things are) and then tied again to steel loops set in the concrete of the tie-down area. The remaining seven also were tied down, but they were tied down in the alleged shelter of a tin-roofed shed.

Well, it wasn't quite that bad; it was enclosed on three sides. Actually, there was one lockable portion of the hangar, but it was not to protect the aircraft. It housed the repair shop, and tools are somewhat more easily stolen than airplanes. I mean, to steal an airplane you have to be able to fly it; but to steal a tool you only have to be able to carry it.

The lockers were inside the repair shop, and they were marked with names, pictures, posters, pinups, bumper stickers, and various other impedimenta collected over the years. Harry told me which one was Slade Blackburn's. I couldn't open it, and I wouldn't have if I could have, because I wanted to be strictly legal. But I did look at it quite closely, and I took notes to be sure that I could adequately identify it on the search warrant I would be going after in about two hours.

Then I went back out to see the plane Harry was looking at. It was nice enough, I suppose, although I couldn't exactly tell the difference between it and Harry's plane except that it might be a little bit newer and maybe a little bigger. "How much does it cost?"

"Oh, well, it's not on the market yet," he said, "but I expect it will be, and I just wanted to have another look at it."

"Why do you think it will be on the market?" I asked idly.

He glanced at me, looking a little apologetic. "Actually, because it was Jack Carson's plane."

"What?" I said, turning my head. "That's no crop-duster!"

"Crop-duster!" Harry exclaimed, sounding outraged. "I should say it's not a crop-duster! It's a Sierra!"

I said that was nice, but I couldn't see why it was particularly different from Harry's plane.

"Good grief!" Harry said. "Look, mine is a Sundowner!"

"Okay," I said.

"This has more seats. It has retractable gear. It has—"

"Never mind," I interrupted, "how much does it cost?"

"Cost?" He glanced at it. "Oh, it'll go for about thirty, thirty-five thousand. Don't worry," he added hastily, "I'm not really going to get it; it's just fun to dream."

"*Thirty*—" I said, feeling dazed. "Wait a minute! How long ago did Jack Carson get that plane?"

"Oh, four or five years ago, why?"

"Did he get it new?"

"Yeah." Harry was looking puzzled, but I think he had begun to realize that right now I was functioning as cop rather than as wife.

"How much did it cost new?"

"I don't know exactly," Harry said. "Something in the neighborhood of sixty thousand dollars. I remember—I should remember the exact date, because he and Slade bought Sierras both the same day, and the rest of us were asking them if they'd robbed a bank or something. They both laughed and Slade said, 'Or something,' and then told us they'd both hit it big in Vegas the same time and decided on the way home to spend the money on fun."

The wheels in my head were turning, and turning fast. I

148

had been wanting a link between Jack Carson and Slade Blackburn; now I'd been given one, and the link, as it had to be, was money. "Was that before or after Jim Baker died?" I asked, certain I knew what the answer would be.

"Well, after, about six months after," Harry said slowly. "Deb, you don't think—"

"Oh yes I do think," I said furiously. "That son of a bitch—" I don't get angry often, but when I do I get very angry, and right now my fists were clenched tightly by my sides. "Show me Slade Blackburn's plane," I added.

Harry showed it to me. It was sitting under the shed, tied down, fueled up, clean, and ready to go. The twin brother to Jack Carson's plane, it was a pretty thing, painted beige and orange with four windows on each side, a wide front window, a polished aluminum nose cone, and, as Harry pointed out enthusiastically, retractable landing gear.

I was absolutely certain that Olead Baker did not know either of these two planes existed.

And I was equally certain that somehow, he had paid for both of them.

11

There are right around eight hundred sworn officers in the Fort Worth Police Department. How is it that I get so lucky? How come, when I called dispatch and told them to send me a backup to serve a search warrant, how come I got Danny Shea?

Look, two weeks ago he was on eleven-to-seven. We have not had a shift change in the meantime. And it was not quite four o'clock when I went back out to the little private airstrip between Beach Street and old Denton Highway to serve that warrant. How did I get Danny Shea?

He wasn't any happier about it than I was.

He told me they had changed his shift, all on account of me. I told him that didn't make sense, and he snorted at me.

"All right," I said, deciding to ignore the snorting, "I won't take up much of your day. This is probably really minor." I showed him a picture of Slade Blackburn; we had gotten it from his personnel file at the bank, which wasn't too happy with him right now. "Now look," I said, "I want you to stand by that plane, right there, and keep an eye out for that man. And if you find him, don't let him go anywhere."

It was just a precaution, you understand. I had no particular reason to suppose Blackburn was going to show up at the airport. No, he didn't think he had gotten away with it—yet. He knew we suspected him; he knew the bank suspected him. He hadn't expected any of that to happen. The bank had invited him not to return to work, and we had searched his house; he had to be scared, some.

But he was a gambler. He ran with Jack Carson, who was a gambler; and he was well enough known as a gambler that his tale of being able to buy a $60,000 aircraft because he had hit it big at Vegas was accepted by his friends; apparently not one of them, including Harry, had stopped to think how unlikely it was that both he and Jack would have gambled lucky at the same time.

The point being, he *was* a gambler; and although the odds on this now weren't as good as he'd expected them to be, I didn't expect him to try to cut his losses and run yet.

Not yet, because if he ran we'd be after him, and if he sat it out and the odds worked for him he could still wind up with—with whatever he'd done it for.

Unless—I'd been told one interesting thing by a man who'd been to Las Vegas with him. "Slade's sharp so long as he's winning," Mark Harper told me. "But he's never learned how to cut his losses. Once he starts to lose, he panics, and then he turns completely unpredictable."

And Mark Harper ought to know. He was a psychology professor at TCU who'd gone on the Las Vegas trips to study the psychology of gambling. He was *very* interested in seeing Olead acquitted; he told me he wished he could help me on that instead of on a bank robbery, which really didn't interest him much at all. I didn't tell him that Slade Blackburn's gambling habits could help very much to acquit Olead.

Panic, I thought. That was interesting. . . . Did he realize yet that he'd started to lose?

Or for that matter, *had* he started to lose yet? I hoped so.

Thus far, the bank examiners weren't sure how much

money was missing. Some of it was in cash, and that was obvious; but some of it would have been taken from ingeniously doctored accounts, inactive accounts, old people's accounts, dead people's accounts, or just any account that nobody was watching closely.

It stood to reason that an account belonging to an insane man would not be too carefully scrutinized, not until that man woke up one morning sane.

Damn it, Olead *had* to have an account there because that was the only way any of this would make sense. Unless I was wrong, unless the two crimes weren't connected at all, unless Slade Blackburn's presence at the party was only a coincidence.

I could not rule that out yet. I am no more immune to error than anybody else, and whatever people may believe, coincidences do happen every day.

It would help if the bank examiners and the computer experts could come up with some names. The FBI had originally estimated ten days to put the files together, but they had now admitted that had been unduly optimistic. Whoever destroyed the files knew exactly what he was going after.

I was sawing steadily at the lock. Its resistance interested me. It was made of case-hardened steel, and even with this hacksaw I was having slow going. None of the other lockers were this secure; Harry's, for instance, had a lock that looked to me as if it had come out of a Cracker Jacks box.

I kept on sawing. My wrists were starting to get tired.

I heard someone yelling—damn, damn, that was Danny Shea yelling, and I heard a shot, and then another shot. I dropped the saw and ran out into the shed, drawing my pistol as I ran.

Danny Shea was standing out on the tie-down area, firing up into the air, and I had to laugh. "Shea," I called, holstering my pistol, "you're not carrying an antiaircraft gun. What happened?"

"The bastard got away," he said excitedly.

"How?"

This one really couldn't be blamed on Shea, I decided after he told me. He had been, obediently if not cheerfully, standing beside Slade Blackburn's plane, or rather walking around Slade Blackburn's plane looking alternately at it and at some others. He said he had vaguely noticed someone glancing in the door of the repair shop, but he hadn't paid much attention until the man walked on out to the tie-down area. Even then he hadn't paid a whole lot of attention; he had watched casually as the man untied the tie-downs on a plane, and only as the man was climbing in did he realize who it was. He had run toward the plane, but by then it was taxiing, and as he drew his pistol the plane took off abruptly from the taxiway without ever entering the runway at all, nearly colliding with another plane as it crossed the landing pattern at an illegal angle.

I radioed in. But Slade Blackburn was gone, and we didn't have any way of chasing him.

It had never crossed my mind that he would take off in somebody else's plane. Keys aren't left in airplane ignitions any more often than they are in car ignitions, and he certainly hadn't had time to hot-wire it. If you can hot-wire a plane. I guess you can.

It wasn't too hard to find the man who owned the airstrip; he had come running out of his office at the sound of shooting, and now he was being profane with Danny Shea, who was also being profane. But he stopped swearing long enough to tell me that no, of course the ignition keys weren't left in that plane.

The plane that was gone, as he told me but I should have already realized myself, was Jack Carson's.

It was quite likely that Blackburn had his own set of keys to Jack Carson's plane.

I went back to the locker, and the owner followed me and said, "Lady, what are you doing? I hope you know that's private property."

I produced my identification, which I had already displayed to his assistant, and showed him the search warrant, which I had also already displayed to his assistant, and he said, "Then why didn't you say so to start with? I'll get that lock off for you."

I told him I would certainly appreciate it if he did, and I stood back and watched as he sliced easily through the metal with some small cutting tool.

Then I opened the locker.

For a minute nobody spoke, and then I got on my radio and said, "Send me a crime scene unit out here."

Looking awed, Shea asked, "Can we count it while we're waiting for crime scene to get here?"

"No, Shea," I told him.

"Why?" he wanted to know, and I explained that we needed crime scene to take pictures of it *before* it was moved.

Then I got back on the radio and told dispatch they better send me an FBI agent, too.

It wasn't as much as it looked like. It turned out to be only $75,000, but being mostly in tens and twenties made it look like more than it was. I wondered what he'd done with the rest of it; there was still a lot of cash showing as out. But it was possible, I thought, that he'd been systematically embezzling for a long time. He was, I had been told by more people than Harry, a high-roller. And it takes money to be a high-roller.

It crossed my mind to wonder why the bank didn't seem to be aware of that reputation, but it seemed he was a man who kept the different parts of his life rigidly compartmentalized. For example, everyone I talked with had agreed his wife had not been at the party. She belonged to a different section of his life.

I had now cleared the FBI's case, but neither of mine looked much better. There was no pistol, and no ammunition, in the locker. Although I now felt morally certain that Slade Blackburn had killed his wife, if I couldn't prove it to a jury then I hadn't cleared the case.

And of course I hadn't definitely proven even to myself that it had been Blackburn who committed the killings Olead Baker was now charged with.

Anyhow, I was supposed to be off duty.

I went home.

About four o'clock Sunday afternoon a dispatcher called me with an update. It seemed that a businessman, landing his plane at Addison Airport, had gone to his tie-down slot and been outraged to find it already occupied. He called the airport authorities, and they ran the registration and found the plane in his slot was the Beechcraft Sierra reported stolen on Saturday in Fort Worth.

The tower had no record of its landing, and no one knew when it had gotten there.

Dispatch said Addison tower wanted to know what I wanted done with it.

After thinking about it, I decided that I wanted somebody from our crime scene unit to go over there and process the plane for fingerprints, so that we wouldn't be dependent only on Shea's testimony as to who it was that took off in it; the Fort Worth Police Department is quite good, and I didn't feel that Shea was likely to be with us too much longer. Also, I called Captain Millner to see what he thought about the advisibility of getting it flown back.

"That would be fine," he agreed, "if we happened to have a pilot. I'm sure there are some in the department, but right off hand I can't think of—"

I told him I could supply one pilot, with about 20,000 hours' air time, who was particularly eager to get behind the controls of that plane, and he said fine, let him fly it back.

So we had the plane back in Fort Worth, and what that accomplished I hadn't, on second thought, the faintest idea. We couldn't compare the lifted latents with known fingerprints of Slade Blackburn because we could not find any on file, and there was no guessing where Blackburn might have gone. He could have stayed somewhere in the Dallas-Fort Worth Metroplex area, or he could have gone just

155

about anywhere in the world, depending on the contents of his billfold.

I wasn't sure how flush that billfold would be. I wondered whether he had any of the missing money with him. I suspected he hadn't; I suspected he'd been trying to pick up his grubstake when he found me sawing his lock open. If I was right, then he would have to reappear eventually, if only to get his hands on his safe deposit box. If he could get to it before we could find it and get a court order to open it. One thing we were sure of now was that it was not in his own bank.

And the other thing we were sure of was that he had one, because we had found the key to it when we went back to search his house the second time. Nobody was sure how it had been missed the first time, as it was in a desk drawer in his den under a stack of papers, not really hidden at all.

It was possible, of course, that it had not been there the first time we searched.

But that was the FBI's problem, and I had no doubt that they would locate the box eventually. They are particularly good with such things as that.

I was to the point of following up small leads now. I talked to everybody I could find who knew Jack Carson or Slade Blackburn; I even dug back in the past to locate people who had known Jim Baker. I talked to everybody in Harry's old flying club, everybody who was still alive and not hiding, which unfortunately amounted to only two people besides Harry.

The trouble was that I didn't know what I was looking for. All I knew was that I needed to find something that would tie Carson and Blackburn together in more than a casual-friends way.

And I didn't get it.

The picture that emerged of Jim Baker—for what it was worth, when Baker had been dead five years—was of an amiable but shrewd good ol' boy. He hadn't had any more money than any of the rest of us did twenty years ago when he joined with Harry and Jack and Slade Blackburn and two other men to buy one old airplane. Well, of course he hadn't, because if he'd been rich then he'd have bought his own plane. He'd had a wife who was a secretary and a six-year-old son who had nightmares.

But he'd been a geologist, and he'd been smart, and he'd been lucky, and in ten years he'd been rich—moderately so.

And then he'd started playing the stock market, and again he'd been smart and he'd been lucky.

The walnut furniture hadn't been old money, as I had guessed; it had been Marilyn's attempt to look like old money.

But Jim had gone on living fairly simply; despite the money, he wouldn't provide his wife with the trips to Vegas, the party life-style, she wanted. He retained his good ol' boy outlook on life; he worked, and he went home and wanted supper on the table and a beer after supper, just as he always had done.

And while Marilyn was upset about the embarrassment of having Olead insane, Jim was worried about the boy. He worked with the psychiatrists all he could; and when it became obvious that Olead (then still called Jimmy) could not function at home even on short trips, Jim tried to find places where he could function. And he wasn't ashamed to be seen in public with a boy—by then, a young man—who was obviously demented.

For Marilyn, that was the last straw. Seven years ago (not eight, as Olead had vaguely remembered) she had sued for divorce. And Texas is a community property state. She married Jack, who was not at all averse to playing party games with the over two million dollars Marilyn wound up with.

Jim, who (read between the lines) was probably more than a little bit tired of Marilyn anyway, shrugged and said the hell with it and went on making money, while Jack and Marilyn industriously went to work seeing how fast they could dispose of two million dollars. By the time Jim Baker, five years ago, crashed his plane into the side of a mountain, Jack and Marilyn were back to living on Jack's income from crop-dusting.

Jack had started spending money again about six months after Jim died, not like he did before, not high-rolling (that word came up again and again) but living comfortably. Some of it I knew the source of; I knew who had bought the house Jack and Marilyn moved into when they moved out of the apartment on Beach Street; but nobody could account for the airplane unless Jack had been telling the truth about winning big at Vegas.

And nobody could quite explain what he'd been living on, as he took on fewer and fewer crop-dusting jobs.

But there was one thing everybody did agree on, and I didn't think it was just because he was dead. Everybody said Jack had a temper; he'd blow up and lash out, and he got in a few fights on account of it, but he'd never set out and plan to harm anybody.

Beyond that, they all agreed he liked to get along with people. He liked people to like him. He was a taker, but he was smooth about it.

The picture that was emerging looked to me like that of a con man. One of his fellow crop-duster pilots put it to me this way: "Jack would steal, but he wouldn't rob. And he wouldn't take the lock off your locker, but if you left the locker open, baby, watch out."

All of which suggested to me he wouldn't have been at all averse to spending money that belonged to his wife's son who probably would never know the difference anyway, but he would have been very unlikely to become involved in murder.

And Slade Blackburn?

Well, nobody seemed to know Slade Blackburn.

Or rather, everybody knew Slade Blackburn, but try to put the pieces together and you'd find out they didn't fit. His fellow pilots were in agreement he was a high-roller.

The people who knew him at the Ridglea Country Club said he was such a gentleman, so attentive to the ladies. And the people at the bank said he was always on time; you could set your watch by him.

His neighbors, for the most part, said they didn't know him. The only man anybody ever saw in his yard was his Mexican gardener.

Gardener . . . that was something I should check on. Were there any other servants?

I found Paco Rodriguez mowing the lawn at a house down the block from the Blackburn house. He told me the señora had hired him to come twice a week to mow the lawn and weed the flower bed. He had never talked to Señor Blackburn, had only seen him once or twice.

He told me the maid was Lupe Sanchez, but he didn't know where she lived.

Do you know how many people there are named Sanchez in Fort Worth? There are 236 in the telephone book, and I was sure there were at least three times that many not listed. I had to look for her, but I decided to call Sanchezes on my own time, from my home telephone.

Finding Slade Blackburn was more urgent, and that I had to do on city time.

Nobody knew where he'd gone. Warrants had been taken by now, and a fugitive bulletin had been issued. He was on TCIC and NCIC, the Texas and national crime information center computers, so that if he was picked up anywhere in the country, for any reason, they'd know he was wanted. But without fingerprints, without a photograph more recent than the five-year-old picture that had been put in his personnel file after the bank's anniversary, when all the employees had been photographed, there wasn't really much anybody could do.

White male. Forty-four years old. Graying, thinning, black hair. Mustache. Fair complexion. Blue eyes. Five feet nine inches tall, a hundred and forty pounds. Smokes Camels. Moderate drinker.

How do you go about looking for somebody meeting that description?

How many of them are there on the street?

Two weeks, and I had been working eight or more hours a day, five or more days a week, and that was all I had . . . well, almost all.

I did, finally, locate Lupe Sanchez.

At first I thought she was going to be no use. We sat in her little apartment off North Main and she told me, in a soft but not very accented voice, that she didn't know Mr. Blackburn. She only worked two days a week, and Mr. Blackburn never came home while she was at work. But then she added, sadly, "It's a shame she got killed when she did. She didn't like that man, and she was going to get away."

"Get away?" I asked.

"Yes. Mrs. Blackburn, she was going to get a divorce. She told me so. She was just deciding what lawyer to call. And she was going to get a lot of money from him, and the house, and all."

Texas is a community property state, with no provision in the law for alimony. She'd have been strictly limited in what she could get, according to the law. So, of course, I asked Lupe what she meant.

"Oh, I don't know. But *she* knew. She told me if he didn't give her what-all she wanted she'd tell what she knew. And then she laughed and laughed. Mrs. Blackburn," Lupe added, "had a very unpleasant way of laughing."

She'd tell what she knew. Oh, really, I thought, and just what *did* she know? Did she, maybe, know where the money to buy the plane really came from?

Maybe Slade wasn't just trying to get rid of her, as I'd guessed. Maybe that murder was another frantic attempt to cover up earlier crimes.

I thought about that one all the way home.

Olead had called Becky every night from Terrell, charging the calls to his telephone credit card—the only credit card he had. He'd given Don a power of attorney to write checks on his bank accounts so that Don could keep his bills paid. Not that he had many himself. The bills were his mother's and his stepfather's. They kept coming, and Don, at Olead's insistence, kept paying them.

The only bills Olead had were for funerals, which he'd arranged by telephone from his jail cell.

He also told Don to pay himself, and Don asked how much. Olead said, "I don't know, how much do lawyers cost?"

Don told him the range, and Olead gave him a figure in the high end of the range. Don told him that was ridiculous; that's not what you pay attorneys fresh out of law school. Olead said, "Why?"

Don tried to explain why.

Olead said, "Look, money is sort of abstract to me, okay? I mean I know I have money in the bank, but I've never had much of a chance to spend any of it myself, and I don't know how much chance I'm going to have in the future. So let me spend it myself right now. You write the check for what I told you to write the check for."

Don said okay, but told him again that was ridiculous.

Telling me about it, he said now he was going to be able to pay the hospital bill when Vicky decided to produce. He'd been worried about it before.

That was on Saturday, and they brought Olead home from Terrell on Sunday afternoon, having kept him a little longer than their tests actually took to give them more time for evaluation.

As we expected, he came home with a unanimous opinion that he was sane enough to stand trial and sane enough to have done whatever he was accused of.

On Monday afternoon at two o'clock, Don called me to inform me, in a tone of voice I didn't like, that he'd just been notified Olead had been indicted.

I said that was impossible.

"It may be impossible," Don said, "but they've sure as hell done it."

"But they *can't*," I said helplessly. "I'd know."

I did some telephoning.

I had taken the warrant. Certainly they should have called me before taking the case to the Grand Jury; in fact, I should have taken the case to the Grand Jury myself.

Only the DA was out with flu—a bad case of flu, one that looked as if it was going to have him laid up for two or three weeks. And his chief assistant had caught the flu from him. The upshot was that a very young assistant DA had decided to rush the case through in flagrant disregard of his office's normal procedure. Because he knew I'd been cooperating with the defense, he'd decided to run the case through the Grand Jury without me.

I tried to call the DA.

His wife said he was too sick to come to the phone.

Look, the DA and I do not always agree on everything, but I knew he didn't want a case in the courtroom before the investigation was completed any more than I did. I called the chief assistant. He coughed a lot over the phone and said he didn't see what he could do about it. He said it certainly wasn't what he would have done, but then it wasn't his case.

I called Captain Millner.

He said the case was in the DA's hands now. But he added, "That supercilious young ass *ordered* me to make you stop working with the defense. I told him I'd never called a detective off an incomplete investigation yet and I wasn't going to start it now. I'll back you all I can, Deb. I'm not ready yet to say he didn't do it, but I'm damn sure ready to say the DA's office has been a sight too precipitous."

I called Don back and told him to do whatever he could think of to get the case continued. The fact that Olead had been indicted certainly didn't mean he had to go to trial yet. In fact, in Tarrant County the delay between indictment and trial was likely to stretch into years; the courts were overcrowded, and there was a crying need for the creation of one or two more districts.

Don answered, "They didn't warn me in law school that there'd be days like this. Well, actually they did, but I didn't quite believe it."

I called the assistant DA who was handling the case, a young fellow named Jerome Lester, and tried to reason with him. "Look, Jerome," I said, as mildly as I could, "I wasn't ready to take a warrant and you decided to take a warrant. I wasn't ready to go to the Grand Jury and you took it to the Grand Jury. Now listen, I'm telling you, this case is not ready to go to trial yet, and if you take it you're going to be embarrassed."

"Now you listen," he said. "You have been deliberately sabotaging this case since day one. You're making a laughing stock out of the whole judicial process. You've been sitting up there in his cell laughing at his dumb jokes and patting him on the back when he starts bawling. Your daughter is running around with him, and your son-in-law is defending him. Well, your brand of justice may be for sale, but mine isn't. Now, have you got anything else to say?"

"Just that he's not guilty," I answered. "I'm not taking a warrant yet because I don't have enough evidence to get a conviction yet, but I'm about ninety-five percent sure I know who did it, and I'm telling you, it wasn't Olead Baker. And as far as justice being for sale, no, mine isn't either, but I think a rich man is just as capable of being innocent as a poor man is. And I think a poor man is just as capable of being guilty as a rich man is. And the other way around. I'm saying don't let's railroad a man just because he's got money. That doesn't make him guilty. It just makes him rich."

"And just how many poor people have you sat up in the jail and talked with? How many poor people have you gone to bat for?" Lester asked nastily.

"More than you think, Jerome," I answered, thinking of some of those times, thinking for instance of a night spent at the hospital sitting beside a gurney in the hall, because all of the emergency rooms were full, watching a drunk woman get an IV pumped into her arm because there were too many people in emergency for anybody who worked there to stay with her, and the doctor refused to let the IV be started unless somebody would agree to stay with her constantly.

After she got two quarts of IV fluid in her, she sat up and announced that she had to go to the bathroom. I took her to the bathroom, and then the doctor decided to come and take a blood alcohol.

It was point four eight.

If I'd just thrown her into the drunk tank and forgotten her, as I was urged to do when she was picked up just as I was due to end my shift, she'd have been dead the next morning from alcohol poisoning.

Who was she?

Just a drunk. I don't remember her name.

But what difference does it make who she was? Or how much money she had? She'd have still been dead.

She was just one person. Just one time. Out of fifteen years.

"Well, I don't have time to talk to you," Jerome Lester said, and I heard the phone slam down at his end, leaving me wondering who his snitch in the jail was.

There's a recent law in Texas requiring trials to be conducted with all possible speed. In vain, the next day, did Don argue in court that that meant all *reasonable* speed.

His request for a continuance was turned down.

Trial was set for Monday.

And none of us were ready.

That gave me a week to find Slade Blackburn, who could be anywhere in the world, and it gave Don a week to prepare a defense for a case that looked open and shut.

12

It was Sunday afternoon, with the trial starting Monday. Becky had spent visiting hours with Olead, but I wanted to see him too once more before facing him in the courtroom. I went over to the jail, and a jailer, with no explanation, led me to the conference room. There were two men there: Don, with stacks of papers, was at the end of the table, and Olead was sitting beside him, his hands clasped on top of a book.

Don looked at me with some annoyance. "Deb," he said, "with all due respect, the cops I don't need right now." I think he still wasn't sure I hadn't known about the Grand Jury.

"Okay," I said peaceably, and turned to go.

Olead stood up. "If she goes, I go," he announced. "I mean, I know I can't go *far*, but—" He shrugged expressively, and Don said something very rude. "You know she's not here as cop," Olead added. "She's here as friend, and God knows I need all of those I can get."

"This is the most cockeyed case I've ever seen," Don fumed, ignoring the fact that he'd seen very few cases thus far. "Damn it, if you intend to conduct your defense yourself, what do you need me for?"

"Are you quitting?"

"No, but—"

"Look," Olead said patiently, "I'm not trying to conduct my defense myself. That's your job, and I'd no more try to do it than I'd try to—to cut my own hair or fill my own teeth. All I'm saying is that we have to play it by my rules."

"Olead, will you listen to me?" Don pleaded. "Will you just listen?"

"I'm listening."

"If you go into the courtroom tomorrow morning the way this case looks right now, you're going to be convicted. I'm telling you, the way you want to fight it, there is no way you can win. And I don't want to have to sit down there in Huntsville and watch somebody put catheters in your arms to pump poison in."

"Then I won't ask you to watch." He glanced at me.

"For heaven's sake, Olead, don't let it happen! You don't have to! I *know* you can get off on an insanity plea no matter what they said in Terrell."

"Susan says I can't," Olead answered stolidly. "Anyway, I'm not insane."

"The hell with that right now, man, we're talking about your *life!*"

Olead turned to face the window, then swung around to face Don again. "That's right!" he shouted. "We're talking about my life. My life, Don, and I'm not going to spend it behind bars. I'd rather die."

"You've got to get some kind of perspective on this," Don argued. "Some system of priorities."

"I've got a system of priorities," Olead answered. "The trouble is you won't respect it."

"Are you firing me?" Don asked. I wasn't sure whether he was asking hopefully or not.

"No, I'm not firing you. Listen, Don. I spent eleven years in and out of a locked room. I'm a healthy man. I've got a healthy body and, right now at least, a healthy mind. But if I get off on an insanity verdict, chances are I won't have a healthy mind long. I could live fifty, sixty more years. And I could live every second of those fifty or sixty years in—you've seen that cell I'm in. You've smelled it. Would you like to spend sixty years in it?"

"It wouldn't be like that," Don argued.

"No, not all the time. I'd be maybe a little free—free to wander around the barred corridors of the prison wing of a state mental hospital, never seeing anything of joy or happiness or love, to live out a gray existence among gray people, to live without hope, without a future or even—dear God—a past. No, Don, I won't live like that. That's one thing. There's another thing that I don't think you've thought about."

"What's that?" Don asked resignedly.

"Just this. You're asking me to say I'm not guilty by reason of insanity. Don't you realize what I'd be saying, by saying that? I'd be standing up in front of God and everybody—literally in front of God and everybody, because I'd be swearing—"

"That's not a sworn statement," Don interrupted.

"*Will you shut up and listen to me!* I'd be saying, yes, I killed my mother and sister and three other people, but it doesn't count because I didn't know I wasn't allowed to, I didn't know it was a wrong thing to do. My God, Don! Would you stand up and say you'd killed your mother and sister?"

Don stared at him, silent. "Well, would you?" Olead demanded again.

Slowly, Don answered, "No, I don't suppose I would."

"You don't suppose you would. Then why are you asking me to?" He slammed his fist down on the table. "Don," he shouted, "look at me. You never look at me when you're talking to me. Do you believe I'm innocent? Do you, Don?"

Don raised his head. Olead's face was flushed; his eyes were blazing. His beard was now an inch long, and his face still bore traces of the beating. Don went on looking at him.

Olead swallowed. "You don't, do you, Don?" he asked, quietly now.

Don dropped his head again. "I don't know, Olead," he said. "God help me, I don't know."

Olead pulled out a chair and sat down. "Well, now I think we're getting at the truth," he said. "If my defense is so bad my attorney doesn't believe it—I guess you'd better make me out a will. Everything to Jeffrey. No. Um—half to Jeffrey and half to TCU, to set up a permanent scholarship fund for premed students who intend careers as psychiatrists and are interested in orthomolecular medicine. I don't think it would be good for Becky for me to leave her anything," he said to me.

I was glad I didn't get a chance to answer, because I was still trying to figure out what to say when Don said, "Olead, damn it—"

"Make the will up anyway. I need to do that. I should have done it a long time ago, only I wasn't of sound mind until six or eight months ago."

I heard a choking sound and looked away from Olead, startled to see Don, his eyes red-rimmed, with his right hand clasped over his mouth.

I think Olead was even more startled than I was. "Hey, I'm sorry," he said. "I didn't mean to—"

"Just hush up, would you?" Don said and swallowed. "Look," he said, "I want to believe you. I *think* I believe you. It's just—damn it, I know what the evidence looks like. I hear you. I know how you feel about Terrell, or wherever you would wind up if you got an insanity verdict. But don't you see, that'd give us more time to look, more time to find evidence—"

"Evidence that might never be found," Olead answered. "I hear you too, Don. I don't like the prospect of the death cell either. But the one certain thing in my life right now is that one day I am going to die. So are you. So are we all. God, I don't know what kind of poison they'd pump into my veins in Huntsville; that's not the kind of thing I keep track of; that's not the kind of thing I *want* to know. It's not supposed to hurt; it's just supposed to be like going to sleep knowing you're not going to wake up. But even if it did hurt—even if it hurt like hell—considering the alternatives, Don, that's the one I've got to choose."

"For a crime you didn't commit."

"For a crime I didn't commit."

"You're either so noble I want to puke, or else you're the biggest coward in Texas. I can't decide which."

"I'm neither," Olead answered. "I'm a man. I want a wife and children and a garden and a cat. I want to go to medical school and be a psychiatrist and do all I can to help keep kids from having to live in the hell I lived in for as long as I lived in it. If I can't have all of that I'll settle for part of it. But if I can't have any of it . . ."

"Then what about the people on the jury, when the evidence to clear you does turn up? What about the executioner?"

Olead shrugged. "That's their problem. I'll be out of it."

Don turned to me. "Deb, can't you make him listen to reason?"

"He sounds quite reasonable to me."

"Deb, you know he's going to be convicted!"

"No, I don't know that," I answered.

Olead chuckled bitterly and said, "Lie a little, why don't you?" He put his hands on my shoulders. "Oh, Mama Hen, Mama Hen, I'm glad I've known you anyway."

I couldn't answer, not right then. I just patted one of his hands, and he stood up straight and said, "All right, Don, what kind of a game plan can we produce?"

"Under your rules, damn little," Don said. "If I bring you a razor, will you shave in the morning?"

Olead thought about it. "No," he said. "I'm just as innocent in a beard as I am without one."

"If I bring you a suit, will you put it on?"

"Definitely. And ditto with some deodorant. And some

decent soap. I think this stuff up here is meant to be laundry detergent."

"If you shave you can have some after-shave," Don said cunningly, and Olead laughed.

"Mama Hen," he said, "will you bring me some men's cologne? I don't think my attorney will."

"What kind do you want?" Don asked resignedly.

"English Leather," Olead said, and turned to me. "Deb," he said, "can you keep Becky away?"

"No," I said, "she has to be here. But she won't be able to be in the courtroom, because she'll be in the witness room."

"Why the hell—" He stopped. "Oh, yeah, the shotgun shell in my bed. Deb, what on earth was Becky doing to find a shotgun shell in my bed? Let me guess. Crying."

"Actually, she was changing the sheets."

"Why was she doing that? Was she expecting me home?"

"Hoping, I think."

"Well, let her know I'll never sleep another night in that house."

"Let her know yourself."

"I can't," he said miserably. "I mean—even if I do, by some miracle, get out of this alive, I'll never sleep in that house again, but—but I also mean—" He stopped. "And she knows it," he said. "We can't talk about that," he explained. "She cries. And I do too. I'm sorry, Deb. I'm really sorry. I never meant that to happen."

"There's nothing to be sorry about," I said.

"Hurting Becky is nothing to be sorry about?"

"Loving Becky is nothing to be sorry about," I said firmly.

"Oh, I know that," he said. "If it was just me loving her it would be okay; she couldn't get hurt by that. But—" He was blinking away tears himself now. "All right. I'm going to be convicted. Barring the miracle of all time, I'm going to be convicted. And—and—the press is going to hound her unmercifully the closer I get to execution. Deb, you know how she feels, don't you? I'm just glad she hasn't had time to *really* fall in love." I wondered who he thought he was kidding with that, as he turned briskly to Don and said, "All I can do is try to get it over with fast. Don, no appeals, you hear me? None."

"Olead, if you won't let me defend you what am I for?"

"Get everything excluded you can. Deb, nobody ever explained to me how that firearms residue test worked, so I couldn't give informed consent, could I? If we could get that kept out of evidence—"

"That and the bruise on your shoulder, we'd be fine," Don agreed. "Only we can't. You were already in custody at that time, and the police department had a legal right to run tests and take photographs."

Olead shrugged. "It was a thought. Go home and get some sleep, Deb."

I went home.

And of course, I did not get any sleep.

I don't remember much about the trial. It was like most trials, except that I didn't spend a lot of time sitting in the witness room before and after testifying. I had signed the warrant and so I had to sit at the prosecution table.

I tried to get out of that. It should have been possible, because Jerome did not want me there any more than I wanted to be there. I knew I had to be in the witness room until I testified, but after that I hoped I could manage to get the court to excuse me so that I could go back to hunting Slade Blackburn.

Gambling, I thought again. He'll be gambling somewhere.

If I was lucky—if he hadn't seen me sawing at his lock, if he'd run only because he saw a police uniform and temporarily panicked—he'd be gambling in the metroplex. And if he was then we ought to be able to find him.

Of course gambling is illegal in Texas. But anybody who

thinks that means it doesn't happen is too naïve to be allowed on the streets.

If he even thought he could come up with any way at all to lay his hands on at least part of the money he'd killed for, he'd be somewhere in the metroplex. I wouldn't be, if I were him, but then I'm not a gambler.

Just a little more time, that was all I needed. But I didn't get it. Judge Key instructed me to take my seat at the prosecution table.

I hated sitting there.

I hated it almost as much as Jerome Lester hated having me there. The judge was pardonably surprised when Jerome announced his intention of treating me as a hostile witness. He even asked me what I thought of that. That gave me the pleasure of telling the judge I was certainly happy Mr. Lester was correct about *something*, as I could not agree with him about anything else I could imagine.

That remark earned me a five-minute lecture from Judge Key on proper courtroom behavior.

Jerome took the witnesses out of order. It was the fourth day before they got to Becky. I remember that Becky cried all the time she was testifying, and after she was through the judge told her she was excused and could go home. They took a five-minute break just then, and Olead, being led back to the holding cell to use the bathroom, stopped in the hall and said, "Becky, please go home."

"Not allowed to talk to the witness," the bailiff intoned as if he had said it thousands of times before.

Becky screamed, "Yes, he can talk to me!"

Olead shrugged and said, "I guess I can't. He's bigger than me, and besides, he has a gun." The bailiff motioned him on towards the holding cell, and he called over his shoulder, quite clearly, "Love you, Becky! Now please go home."

Becky choked, "I love you too, Olead." But the steel doors had slammed shut.

He didn't hear her.

She went home but didn't stay; instead, she went and got Vicky and returned to the courtroom, and she and Vicky were there again, despite my pleas that she stay home, as the trial went on into its fifth day.

When we recessed for lunch on Friday—with me still not having been called—I ran for a phone. By now I'd involved the Metro Intelligence Squad and cajoled them into checking into every known gambling location in the metroplex and looking for new ones. At every break I called them again. I was sure they were sick of me, but I wasn't about to give up.

Not yet.

Not ever.

And I wasn't going to have to, because a Dallas lieutenant named Carl Weston told me they'd picked up Slade Blackburn at ten o'clock Thursday night in a surprise raid on the very interesting back room of an exclusive North Dallas night spot. It had taken this long to identify him, he said, because Blackburn had had no identification on him. He hadn't acted scared, and he'd given the name of Hollowell, but Weston thought he looked familiar, and when "Mr. Hollowell" refused to give his address Weston had called the president of the bank to come over and look at him.

I asked when we could get him back to Fort Worth, and Weston told me as soon as I could come get him. I was tied up in court, I explained, and would have to send someone else.

Then I called the captain.

We'd have Blackburn in Fort Worth by late afternoon . . . for all the good it wouldn't do now, because nobody was going to let me stop the trial to let the defendant have a look at a new suspect.

I went to look for Don, to get him to ask for a continuance, but I couldn't find him. Having no idea where he'd go for lunch, I checked every restaurant in walking distance of the courthouse. At two o'clock I raced back to the court room, getting there just in time to keep Judge Key from chewing me out for being late.

In retrospect, I wonder if perhaps I was not at least halfway in shock throughout the trial. I remember looking at Olead and wishing I could look away while I was describing the bruise on his shoulder, and I remember telling of watching the ident tech swab his hands for gunpowder residue. I remember the quiet, grave look on Olead's face while I described that.

Don, being a proper defense attorney, asked me about the two red paper shotgun shells, and I testified that we had not been able to locate any red paper shotgun shells in the house except for the empties. He asked me if that had caused me to reach any conclusions and of course the prosecution attorney jumped up and objected. They wrangled about it a while and the judge ruled the defense could not ask that question.

They argued some more, and finally decided he could ask me where the red paper shotgun shells came from. I said they must have been brought from outside the house, probably already loaded in the gun. The prosecution attorney objected. The judge sustained the objection and cautioned me to do no more theorizing.

The defense asked me if I knew whether Olead had bought any shotgun shells, and I said I had not been able to discover that he did. On redirect, the prosecution asked me whether I had made any effort to determine whether the defendant could have purchased any shotgun shells, and of course I had to say that I had not. The defense let me explain that paper shotgun shells have not been produced for about twenty years. The prosecution objected. The judge decided to allow that answer to stand.

The defense let me tell how Olead had mourned over his sister's body, and how he had cried the next day over the bag of marbles.

But there was no way around the bruise on his shoulder and the firearms residue on his hands, and the fact that I could prove there was a sixth shot did not prove he had not fired the other five, particularly when the firearms examiner testified that the other shotgun had jammed after the fourth shot—a fact nobody had ever told me.

I had one hope left, and it was a crazy one. If we could get a mistrial—

What could we do to get a mistrial?

I couldn't do anything; the judge was already mad enough at me. No, Don or Olead would have to do it, whatever it was, and I had to think fast.

I thought fast. And all I can say in defense of what I thought up was that maybe I was a little bit in shock. There was no real reason to assume it would work. But I couldn't think of anything else.

At the next recess, I went hunting a deputy who owed me a favor. I found Clint Barrington, and told him what I wanted, and he said, "Deb, you're nuts."

"Look, Clint, I—"

"Debra, you are positively out of your gourd."

Nobody, but nobody, is allowed to call me Debra. I reminded him of that and he laughed. "Deb, is it really that important?"

I told him it was really that important.

"If I wind up getting in trouble over this shenanigan—"

I told him I'd take the blame.

"I'm not promising," he said. "But I'll try. Okay? That's the best I can do. I'll try."

At seven-fifteen the jury retired to consider its verdict. It was really getting late for that; they ought to have broken for the night if not for the weekend, but the judge wanted the next week off. He was determined to finish Friday night if he had to keep the court in session until midnight.

I was worried about Vicky by now; her face was showing strain, but she insisted on staying as long as her sister stayed, and Becky wouldn't leave. Harry had come to join them at six, but he left when the jury left, to go and check on Hal. He said he'd be back after seeing to it Hal had eaten supper and settled down.

The rest of us went on waiting.

After about thirty minutes of deliberation, the jury brought in a verdict of guilty. Becky began to cry; I glanced back to see Vicky hugging her, but I couldn't go to them, because I was still sitting at the prosecution table. So I sat, feeling numb, hearing Don whisper, "I told you we should have gone for an insanity plea. Damn it, Olead—"

Olead answered, "And I told you why I didn't want to. Can I address the jury?"

"What do you want to do that for?"

"Well, you said they had to consider the sentence, and I want to ask them for—"

"That will be totally unnecessary," Don told him gloomily.

"Then can I tell them I'm not mad at them and I don't have any hard feelings toward them?"

"You can do that after the sentence."

Olead shrugged.

The judge explained this portion of the trial to the jury, and again they were not out over half an hour. They came back with the expected sentence: death by lethal injection.

And just for a moment I let myself despair. I had done all I could, and it hadn't done any good. Barrington had let me down on what was probably a fool's idea anyway, and Olead wouldn't let Don appeal. Maybe even, in that one moment, I thought, damn it, what if he *did* do it? I still didn't have any explanation of the firearms residue on his hands, the bruise on his shoulder—but then I looked at Olead again and knew again that he couldn't have done it.

Yes, maybe he had killed Jack—that was a good possibility—and if he had then he'd had a good reason to kill Jack. And maybe he'd fired at somebody else, somebody I was now sure would have been Slade Blackburn, but if he did he'd had a good reason for that, too. But he didn't kill Brenda. And he didn't kill his mother.

Olead was going to die for a murder I felt morally certain he had not committed, and there was nothing I could do to prevent it.

I shouldn't be mad at the jury. No, they weren't out long; the case looked open and shut, and it was late and we hadn't had over a ten-minute break since lunch; why should they stay out long? But I remember thinking bitterly, yes, this is it, Olead dies so the jury can go home and have supper.

I do not remember getting up and walking around Jerome Lester to get to Olead. But I must have, because I had him in my arms, and I was crying, and he said, "Don't, Deb, don't, at least I'll die sane." But his arms around me clung desperately. He didn't want to die.

He didn't want to die, but he wouldn't let Don appeal, because even less than he wanted to die did he want to stay alive without hope.

The judge was pounding his gavel and shouting for order, and one bailiff was heading towards me, to get me back where I belonged; and Clint Barrington, behaving as if he thought this case entirely concluded, was bringing in another prisoner to be arraigned. I wanted to scream, "What took you so long?" But I didn't say anything. I just watched, and I noticed vaguely that Slade Blackburn had lost weight.

Olead was watching too; his head was turning like an alert bird dog, watching Barrington, watching Blackburn, and he backed very slightly away from me. All at once I felt him stiffen, and I could no longer hear his breath at all. Then his hand went under my jacket and he said, "Sorry, Deb, I need this."

He had my gun, and a lot of people were shouting all at once. A bailiff and Clint Barrington and another deputy sheriff made abortive jumps toward him and then they all froze, because by then he had grabbed Slade Blackburn, and the muzzle of my pistol was under Blackburn's chin. Olead turned, dragging Blackburn, and backed up to the judge's high podium so that nobody could get behind him. "Now I remember!" he shouted. "I've never fired a gun in my life, but even I couldn't miss at this range. It was you! Now I remember."

I wanted him to recognize Blackburn. That was all I wanted. Just recognize him and tell Don. Not grab a gun, not— I thought, despairingly, what have I done? He's snapped again—Susan was wrong when she said he wouldn't—

But he looked sane. He looked unbelievably angry, he looked like a man who had just discovered what anger was for, but he looked sane.

"How did you drug me, bastard?" he demanded. "That's the first step. It was in the punch, right?"

And it couldn't be happening, nobody would really answer like that, but Slade Blackburn answered him. "Damn right it was in the punch! I'd had the stuff for years; your old man left it out at the airstrip one day when he'd had you out there, and you so gaga you didn't know what an airplane was. Oh, you were so damn easy, you even said the punch didn't taste right and your mother told you to drink it anyway—so damn weak, twenty-six years old and not the guts to tell mama no—"

Olead swallowed. "And I remember—there was a loud noise in the hall, and I got up and went to the bedroom door, and you were there, and you said, 'It's okay, I'm going hunting with Jack and we're just getting ready,' and I was so sleepy I went back to bed. What was it, what was that noise, was that when you shot Brenda?"

"Yes, damn you!" Blackburn screamed. "Let go of me, you're choking me!"

"God knows I'd like to choke you!" Olead shouted. "But I'll let go of you just as soon as we've got this settled. You came into my room later and put the gloves in my jacket pocket and the baseball shoes back on the floor, and then you leaned over me and opened my window and shoved the screen off, and you sat me in bed and put the shotgun to my shoulder and pointed the barrel out the window and put my finger to the trigger and you fired with your hand wrapped around my hand, so that I'd have a bruise on my shoulder, so that I'd have gunpowder on my hands, and then you left, counting on it there was still enough of the drug left in my system that I'd go on sleeping and not remember, and I didn't remember, not until I saw you—damn you, damn you, damn you, why did you do it, why?"

"It doesn't matter! Go on and kill me; it's too late now anyway—"

"You're damn right it's too late, but you're going to tell me *now*."

I couldn't see what Olead's left hand was doing, but Blackburn wriggled and squealed and said, "I'll tell, let go! All right—you had money—in my bank—"

"In your bank? What bank is that?" He should remember. I'd told him. No, I'd asked him.

"First Federated of Ridglea—you had nearly three-quarters of a million—"

"No, I didn't."

"Yes, you did! And you didn't even know it. Your daddy set it up before the divorce went through, put it in your name rather than his, so there'd be something left no matter what that dippy dame cost him. He wanted to be sure you would have a keeper all your life. And he never told you about it. I realized that, because I talked with other bankers, and in the first two months after your daddy died there was activity on every other account you had, but there was no activity at all on this one—"

"So you used it."

"You weren't supposed to know! You wouldn't have known—if you'd did like you should've—but when Jack asked me to the party he told me about you. And he was getting antsy, he and I had split the money and he'd hidden the statements when the computer kicked them out and sent them back to you, but he was worried, he was thinking about telling you—he said you'd protect him, for your mother's sake—but I knew damn well that wouldn't go for me—"

"Jack said he was worried about money, that night," Olead said slowly. "I wish I'd known—all right. Tell me, then. How much did you and Jack take, all told?"

"I don't know."

"I asked a question, and I want an answer," Olead said savagely, and Blackburn squealed again. "I didn't mean to the penny. Give me an estimate. How much did you take?"

"Maybe—maybe five hundred thousand."

"Leaving me over four million. You took five hundred thousand dollars that I didn't need or even want. Well, you can have it, bastard, you can have every penny I've got, if you can give me back my sister. But you can't do that, can you? Was it fun? Did you enjoy pumping a load of buckshot into the back of a sleeping four-year-old? Did you enjoy killing—the only person who ever loved me?"

Abruptly, he let go of Blackburn and kicked him hard, and Blackburn fell against the prosecution table and hastily crawled under it. Barrington went to get him out, but stopped when he saw Olead still had the pistol in his hand. Olead turned and handed the pistol back to me, and I put it in my holster and slapped him as hard as I could. I had stopped crying by then, and I screamed, "You blithering idiot, how dare you say Brenda was the only person who ever loved you?"

He put his hand to his face, looking dazed, and said, "What?"

"What about your daddy? What about your brother? What about Susan? What about Becky? What about *me*? Do you think I have to give birth to a child to love that child? I told you I was a mother before I was a cop, but I never gave birth to a child in my life. All my children are adopted. I never saw you till New Year's Day, but that doesn't mean I don't love you."

He stared at me, silently, as I raged on. "Damn it, that was totally unnecessary! All you had to do was tell Don or me and we'd have taken over from there; that verdict wouldn't have held, not with proof someone else did it, and the FBI says the bank records will be put together in a few more days. You could have gotten yourself killed right here in this courtroom, trying to play Perry Mason. Now go and sit down and don't you ever grab a gun from me again!"

He went and sat down, his arms down on the defense table and his face hidden in his arms, and the judge was pounding with his gavel and demanding order again, a demand which at this point sounded idiotic. But I went out to the spectators' area and sat down, because I couldn't stand to sit at the prosecution table again, and Barrington finally got Slade Blackburn out from under the table and out of the courtroom, and at last the courtroom got quiet again except for the reporters. A cold stare from the judge silenced that area, too.

Panic, I thought. This was what that psychology professor meant, I'd just seen it happen, Blackburn's panic at the thought of losing. For this panic, six people had died, and Olead could have—Olead could have. He'd meant Olead to die.

Becky was pulling at my arm, saying something I didn't really notice. I said, "Just a minute, Becky."

"But Mom—"

"Just a *minute*," I repeated.

The judge said something, I don't remember what, and Don and Jerome went to the bench. Jerome looked as if he couldn't decide whether to faint or throw up. They stood and talked with the judge a while. I heard Jerome say, "Yeah, but—" two or three times, but he never got any further. He shook his head a few times and nodded once. Don was talking too quietly for me to hear him, except once when he said, "Yes, sir." It appeared that the judge was doing most of the talking. I couldn't hear much of what he said, but Jerome seemed very upset about it.

Someone in the jury box was crying.

Judge Key, looking extremely angry, said, "Ladies and

gentlemen of the jury, in view of recent developments, I am setting aside your verdict. I hereby declare this a mistrial." He looked at Jerome. "Mr. Lester, do you have anything you wish to say?"

"Yes, sir, I—er—the state wishes to—er—drop all charges. Sir." He sounded as if he had been inadequately coached and was afraid of forgetting his lines.

Someone else in the jury box started crying.

The judge looked at Olead and said severely, "You have displayed extreme contempt of court. But the district attorney's office has agreed not to file any charges for your disgraceful conduct, and considering the mitigating circumstances, I shall say no more about the matter. This court has dismissed all charges. You are excused."

Don stood up and said over the ensuing pandemonium, "Your honor, my client's brother has been temporarily placed in a foster home. Do you know of any reason why he cannot now be placed in the custody of my client?"

"Mr. Howell, you will have to draw up a formal custody petition," Judge Key said. "However, I have no objection to the child being—er—allowed to visit his brother until such time as a custody hearing can be scheduled."

Becky slipped past the bailiffs to Olead. With one arm around her, he looked around eagerly, and seconds later Jeffrey was in his other arm. Wiping tears out of her eyes, the foster mother said to me in a confidential tone, "The poor mite was fretting so for Oyee I just couldn't believe he ought to be kept away. So I brought him up here to wait for the verdict. I just knew it would be like this. Anybody one baby would love that much wouldn't hurt another baby."

"Mom," Vicky said, in a rather frantic tone, and I turned to see her standing right beside me. She was very pale, and she looked past me. "Don," she said, "I think I need to go to the hospital *now*."

Don looked at the judge. He looked at his watch. Then he said, "Uh—can it wait just a minute?"

"*No!*" Vicky said, both hands on her midsection. "It's already been waiting an hour. I need to go *now!*"

"Oh, shit," Don said, and then he said, "Sorry, Vicky, I didn't mean you. But somebody's got to get Olead back up to the jail—"

"What for?" Olead demanded.

"To get processed out."

Jerome Lester said, "I'll handle that, if you'll trust me to it. Or he can wait and come back Monday, if you'd rather—"

"We'd rather," Don said, and he and Vicky left fast.

I'd have to let the captain know the outcome before I could join them, I sternly reminded myself; and I walked with Olead and Becky and Jerome out into the hall.

The process of justice continued in its normal orderly fashion. Barrington, with an expression saying he'd have lots to say to me later, was leading Slade Blackburn back toward the courtroom for arraignment.

Olead stopped to let them pass, and for a moment they looked at each other, Olead with Jeffrey riding on his left hip, and his right arm around Becky, and Slade Blackburn alone in handcuffs, looking at him like a beggar looking in the window.

Just for a moment they looked at each other, and then Olead walked past him and down the corridor. I offered my car keys to Becky, but she told me she had her own. I stopped by a phone and called the captain, and then I called home, and then I went on to the hospital.

At eleven o'clock, Harry unlocked the front door and I turned on the living room light. The TV was on, but not loud, and I could hear rather muffled rock music from the closed door of Hal's bedroom.

My living room seemed to have acquired a playpen. A baby was in it, asleep, in a red romper suit. Becky was asleep on the couch, and Olead was asleep in Harry's recliner chair, with my cat in his lap and his hand on the cat. Becky sat up when the light came on. Olead didn't sit up, but he opened his eyes, smiled, and began to pet the cat.

Who purred.

Hal's door swung open, and the rock music immediately

became louder as Hal dashed out into the unlit hall, looking somewhat more Korean than usual as he stood in the shadow. In fact, he is somewhere between a fourth and a half Korean, the rest being, presumably, American GI. Very loudly, he demanded, "Did Vicky have twins?"

"No," Harry said tiredly, "she had a very big boy. Nine pounds fourteen ounces. They've named him Barry."

"That sounds little to me," Hal said.

"That's huge, dummy," Becky told him indignantly.

Olead had been staring at Harry. "I know you," he said slowly. "I remember. Dad took me out one day flying and you were there, and you said that one day you'd teach me to fly a helicopter. Your name—your name is Harry. I remember. I didn't know you were Becky's dad."

"That's right," Harry said. "That's been—what, ten, twelve years ago? You ready to learn?"

"I think I'd better learn to drive first," Olead said. "And I hope you don't mind if Jeffrey and I stay here tonight. I'll find an apartment tomorrow, but I didn't want to start looking tonight."

I asured him we didn't mind, and Harry said the same thing, and Olead smiled. "I know you don't," he said, "but I had to ask anyway."

The cat stood up, stretched, looked pointedly at the light, and yawned. Then it lay back down in approximately the same position, and Olead scratched its ears. "Cats know when it's bedtime, don't they, fella?" he said, and went on scratching its ears.

The cat purred.

I think maybe so did I.